FOLLOW THIS INTRIGUING CAST OF CHARACTERS —
BEAUTIFUL CO-EDS, BOOKISH PROFESSORS, WISTFUL
SHOP-GIRLS, ARTISTS AND ONE ASTONISHING NYM-
PHET — THROUGH ONE OF THE MOST ENTERTAINING
NOVELS TO EXPLODE INTO PRINT IN A LONG, LONG
TIME.

"Admire Smith's dexterity . . . his sure sense of the absurd . . . it's
a virtuoso performance."

William French
Globe & Mail

". . . a cornucopia of fascinating, penetrating character studies
. . . this simultaneously sensitive and outrageous treatment of the
human condition places this novel easily among the most suc-
cessful in this particular mode . . ."

Windsor Star

". . . absurd . . . delightful . . . wit and sharp satirical sense."

Canadian Literature

". . . compulsive reading, deeply moving and unique in Canadian
writing."

Montreal Gazette

". . . savour a literary experience rarely encountered. Smith has an
extraordinary ability to catch individual voices . . . an elegant and
accomplished stylist."

The Atlantic Provinces

"(Ray Smith) is an assembler of worlds miraculously complete . . .
he's an explorer of shadows and substances, of hard realities and
fabulous conducts."

Books In Canada

"*Lord Nelson Tavern* is a convincing performance."

Robert Fulford
Toronto Star

Ray Smith is beginning to command attention as one of Canada's most promising writers. His work has been published by *Maclean's, Tamarack Review, Prism* and *Journal of Canadian Fiction* and his short stories have been included in eight major anthologies.

Smith's previous book, *Cape Breton is the Thought Control Centre of Canada*, was recognized as one of the best Canadian books published in 1969.

He was born in 1941 in Cape Breton and graduated from Dalhousie University. He currently lives in Montreal which he describes as "a beautiful city and the home of the world's most beautiful women".

Ray Smith

Lord Nelson Tavern

General Editor: Malcolm Ross

New Canadian Library No. 158

McClelland and Stewart

Quotation from "Stand by Your Man"
B. Sherrill & T. Wynette, courtesy of
Al Gallico Music Corp.

The Canadian Publishers
McClelland and Stewart Limited
25 Hollinger Road, Toronto

Manufactured in Canada by Webcom Limited

Books by Ray Smith

Cape Breton is the Thought Control Centre of Canada
Lord Nelson Tavern

1

Two Loves

Everyone was in love with Francesca. Afternoons they would skip classes to sit around the tavern talking about her, her beauty.

"Her eyes, now, her eyes are the mystery of the universe, the light of day, the movement of music, the . . . the . . . ."

"Her legs, Gould, her legs have the elegant curves of an eagle's flight, of a beach shimmering in the sun, of . . . ."

"For Christ's sake," from Naseby, "the important thing is how good a lay she is."

No one knew this, for none of them had ever spoken to her, not even Ti-Paulo the painter whose sexual successes were legendary. "I'm not interested in princesses," he said with a smirk as he went off to paw a third year sculpture student.

They tried gathering information about her: her name, what classes she was in, then, amazingly, her faculty.

"Science, for God's sake. Incredible. A fucking physics major. What a fucking waste."

Gloom. They had no openings. Gould and Paleologue were in English, Naseby in philosophy (something few of them remembered in later years), Grilse in economics, Ti-Paulo in the art school a few blocks away. They had cut themselves off from the science students, though it seemed it wouldn't have done them much good anyway, for the science students were as much in awe of Francesca as they were.

"Hey, hey, I've just heard, she's Venezuelan and her father gave her an oil well for her eighteenth birthday, and . . . hey, you guys aren't interested anymore, is that it?"

Gould was annoyed; it wasn't often he was first with some gossip. Paleologue explained.

"I heard this morning that she's the adopted daughter of a Greek shipping magnate and she was given a yacht on her eighteenth birthday. Naseby found out last night that her father was a Russian prince who moved to Brazil and died there and that her step-father owns a million acres of coffee plantation; she was given her own little jet last Christmas; we note that she does belong to the school flying club. Grilse here heard from a girl in her residence that Francesca is illegitimate and that the Italian Ambassador to France sends her jewellery on all special occasions. It comes rather mysteriously by diplomatic courier. So you see, my dear Gould. . . ."

Further gloom.

"Perhaps all the stories are true."

"Perhaps none of them are; perhaps she's the daughter of an illiterate contraceptive king from Gary, Indiana . . . ."

Paleologue solved the problem, though without satisfying anyone: "Perhaps she's just the sort of girl legends get told about." Paleologue was a poet.

They ordered another gloomy round.

But there was more that fall than thinking about Francesca. It was a year of friendship (they were all years of friendship then), a year of thinking and growing, a year of love. It was the year Paleologue was going with Lucy, the year Gould met Rachel. Later in the winter it was Naseby and Nora. Even Ti-Paulo took time off from screwing his way through the art school to spend two weeks with a girl from the phys. ed. department. Probably Grilse was going with someone, but with Grilse you never knew.

Paleologue's Lucy was a surprise to everyone, especially Paleologue and Lucy themselves. She was a delightful girl, light and airy, blonde and blue-eyed, thin, the ethereal thinness of the tuberculoid or the chronically undernourished. She was a typist and had come to town from a little place forty miles away. "Just a kinda wide place on the road, you know what I mean? Really awful, boy, I couldn't wait to get away from there, nothing to do but get pregnant and watch the trucks go by. I was going to join the air force for a while, and off and on I thought maybe I'd be a nun, the nuns at school they keep at you, you know, and a little place like that, I mean, it's all right, but you gotta get out if you have any ambition, you know, you want to make something of yourself, you have to do it because no one's going to do it for you, right? And, well, there was this guy, we were going to get married and I wanted to earn some money first, it costs a lot to set up a house these days, but . . . well, I guess I'll just put it in the bank and hope . . . I mean, I suppose I shouldn't be telling you about this but . . . well, Jackie was really a great guy in some ways, you'd like him, you really would, he could make you laugh, we had a lot of really great times together, dances and parties, that's one thing about living in the city, you don't find parties like that around here, everyone's so cold, just a lot of strangers, but back home we used to . . . well, anyway, what was I . . . oh yeah, I was going to tell you about Jackie, this'll really kill you. See, we were at a party at my friend Joyce's, Joyce used to have really great parties, everyone always had a great time, and there was this girl, Peg-O, that's what we used to call her till she was about fourteen, then we started calling her Pig-O, for the obvious reasons, you know what I mean? Gee, I haven't thought about her for so long, I think she went away somewhere, it got too hot for her, oh meow, aren't I terrible, if you can't say something good about a person, anyway, Pig-O, I shouldn't call her that, Peg-O was tall and thin and she wasn't what you'd call good looking or anything, but she had these legs, she was really proud of them, always wore the shortest skirts around, anyway, that night she was sort of playing around with these two guys, playing one off against the other and they were getting sort of teed off with her, I mean, you do that sort of thing and after a while people get kind of tired of you, right, so these guys got together in the kitchen and sort of talked it over and decided nuts to

Peg-O, they'd take a bottle and go for a ride and get drunk together and that would show her. And it sure did, boy was her nose ever out of joint, she was fit to be tied and started insulting everyone, even poor Joyce which is really bad manners if you ask me, so anyway Jackie, he never had much use for her anyway, knowing him it was him that started calling her Pig-O, that's just like him, God, I'll never tell you what he used to call me, but never mind that, Jackie decided to take her down a peg or two, if you'll pardon the expression, aren't I awful, anyway, he got this look in his eyes, he was a real devil when he got like that, and this was when John F. Kennedy was still alive and there were pictures of Jackie Kennedy all over everywhere, so he looks at Peg-O and he says, 'Hey Pig-O,' he was the only one who could call her that to her face, 'Hey Pig-O,' he says in the sweetest voice you ever heard, butter wouldn't melt in his mouth, 'I've just noticed,' he says, 'I've just noticed you've got feet like Jackie Kennedy.' What a scream, you should have seen the look on her face, like . . . no, wait . . . no, I can't do it . . . anyway, we're all pretending we're not noticing a thing, you know and splitting our sides, and Peg-O says, 'What do you mean, I have feet like Jackie Kennedy?' and he says, 'Well, you've seen pictures of Jackie Kennedy, haven't you?' and she says, 'Of course I have, you think I live in a cave or something,' and he says, 'Well, you know what her feet look like?' and she says, 'No, I can't say I've ever noticed Jackie Kennedy's feet, for Christ's sake,' and he says, 'Well, you take a look at Jackie Kennedy's feet and you'll see what I mean,' and she says, 'What the hell are you talking about, what are you trying to say about my feet?' and he says, 'I was just trying to say your feet look like Jackie Kennedy's feet,' and she says, 'You leave my feet out of it,' and he says, 'What are you getting all steamed up about, I'm only saying you should get a picture of Jackie Kennedy and take a look at her feet,' and she says, 'You can take Jackie Kennedy and her feet and you can all go take a long walk on a short wharf,' and . . . oh, it was a real riot, I think my sides were sore for three days after that, and the funniest thing was, her feet really did look like Jackie Kennedy's feet, that's the kind of guy he was, you know, he noticed things . . . though

I suppose you could say that was the trouble with him, he noticed too many things, like other women, for example. . . . It's funny isn't it, I mean, I guess I still love him in a way, but what he did to me, I almost hate him too, you know what I mean? See, what happened was this, we'd been going together for about three years and then at Christmas he . . . well, the way it was, he was over to our place Christmas morning for opening our presents, you know, and I opened mine and it was that purse I have, you know, the one with the sequins, and I said, hey, that's really nice, I really needed a party purse, and he says, look inside it and I did and I nearly had a bird, there was this box and it was a diamond, boy what a fuss that caused, I mean, I'd sort of been expecting it, but Jackie was always able to surprise you, and anyway, that was . . . a year ago last Christmas, and I was still in school so I wanted to put it off for a while so I could, like I say, work for a year in town so we'd get a bit ahead, so when I got my grade eleven I came into town and got a job, and I would go home on weekends. It wasn't the best arrangement, I mean I would have preferred working right there, but there just wasn't any work, I mean, have you ever heard of a girl gas jockey? and I sure wasn't going to work in the snack bar, no way, so even if I had to be in town all week that was all right, even if he was doing some running around, because I figured it was better for him to get it out of his system first, boys will be boys, you know what I mean, but there are limits, I mean, I never minded if he wanted to go fooling around during the week, that's fine so long as I don't know about it, what you don't know won't hurt you, right, but on the weekends, boy, there can't be any monkey business, I mean that's only fair, isn't it, I'm his girl, his fiancée, right, so when I'm home, if he really cares about me then he's going to spend his time with me and that's it, I mean, it's the least you can expect. So anyway, last Christmas, I was home for . . . let's see, Christmas was a Monday, right, so I was home from Friday afternoon until Tuesday night, and it was going to be a really nice time because this was the first Christmas I really had any money of my own, well, enough to buy some really nice presents for people and I was able to do all my shopping in town and besides that it was going to be sort of the anniversary of our engagement and I'm like a little kid when it comes to birthdays and anniversaries and Christmas, you know what I mean, so anyway, I get home on Friday evening and we go out together and same thing Saturday, and then on Sunday—that was Christmas eve—we were supposed to go over to Joyce's, she was just having a few of us over, but I knew there was something wrong between me and Jackie, there was something going on, you know how you get this feeling, there's nothing you can pin down or anything, just . . . you know. Of course I asked him what it was, was there anything wrong, and of course he said there wasn't and stupid me, I believed him, he could charm the spots off a leopard, but then Sunday night, Christmas eve, what a time to have your engagement go up the spout, eh, Jackie was supposed to pick me up at seven and I was all dressed and ready, you know how I am about being ready on time, and seven comes and no Jackie. Well, that was okay, but then it was seven thirty, and then eight, and still no Jackie and my mother is saying, well, perhaps he had to work late and I said, what kind of work would he have on Christmas eve, he worked in a lumber yard and, sure, they sold Christmas trees, but only for shipping into town, everyone out there just goes out and chops one down, so he wasn't at work, I knew that. So anyway, I'm sitting around, dressed to the nines, boy you men are so lucky, you don't have to just sit waiting for someone to come and pick you up and if you call and ask you're a nag, boy if I was a man, anyway, it's eight thirty and I'm just about out of my tree and I knew he wasn't still at work and I wondered, is he out with the boys and just forgot, but I didn't think so because, have you ever noticed, there are two kinds of men, the ones who like boozing with the boys and the ones who go after women, it's true, you look around you sometime, anyway, Jackie wasn't the drinking sort, not that he wouldn't take a drink, I don't mean that by a long shot, but he could take it or leave it, so if he was that late, then it had to be a woman, that's just the way he was. So I started trying to figure out who it could be and I went over everyone he'd ever gone out with that I knew about, trying to figure out who was home for the holidays and whether they were going with someone else and whether he was still interested and it was really hard, because he was always careful and of course no one was telling me anything even if they did know, the woman is always the last one to find out. Anyway, I was going over all these names and I was trying to remember what he'd said about them, because I was always asking him to tell me the gossip, you know, and he would say, oh, Patsy is going with Bill, and Rita is going with this guy over in Duck Lake, and it was like he was saying, okay, I used to go around with Rita but I can't be now, can I, because she's going with this guy, right, so then I figure, thinking all the time there, Lucy, the one to watch for is someone he hasn't mentioned at all or someone when I asked about her he would say, oh, I don't know, haven't seen her around much, maybe she's seeing some married guy on the sly, and that would be the one, and as soon as I thought that it came to me in a flash, what about Dianne Hackett, she's still around and Jackie was really stuck on her for a while about two years earlier but they broke up, but the thing was, he never told me much about why they broke up, just something like, oh, you know how it is, so I bet he still cares for her, right, so it has to be Dianne, I knew, I just knew it was her, so I borrowed my brother Sonny's car and said I was just going to get some cigarettes and started over to Dianne's place, boy I was just shaking like a leaf, I was so nervous, you know, not wanting to be right, but wanting to know and so on, so anyway, I'm coming up to her place and there's this car out front and sure enough it's Jackie's car and the two of them in the front seat, not necking or anything, she was over by the door, but still, so anyway, I had him and I didn't know what to do about it so I just kept on driving till I came to the gas station, it was closed by that time, thank God, and I stopped and just broke right up, you know, I was really sick, I didn't know what to do, I mean that's it, right, game over, and when that happens . . . but anyway, I got hold of myself and decided I'd better do something fast, like in case they recognized Sonny's car, so I started back down the road and, thank God, or maybe not thank God, I don't know, anyway, they were still sitting there, so I drove up and stopped right beside him, I was facing him now so the two driver's

15

sides were right together, and I rolled down the window and just looked at him, you should have seen the look on his face, he knew I had him this time, and he started to roll down his window, and I just took off my glove and just looking him straight in the eye I pulled off the ring and held it out and when he reached out his hand I just dropped it, you know, before his hand got out to mine and it fell right there on the road you know, and the snow and all and he was just saying, 'Hey Lucy,' or something and I gunned it out of there because I didn't want to hear anything or I'd have broken up again and I was darned if I was going to cry in front of her and I sure was going to cry and I wanted to do that at home in my room with the door closed. So that was it, well, it wasn't really, because as soon as I got home he called and said he wanted to explain and I said, what is there to explain, you were an hour and a half late and you were sitting in the car with Dianne Hackett and he said there was nothing between them, and I said, well that's too bad isn't it, Dianne's about my size, the ring would probably fit her, he'd be able to get two Christmas presents out of it, me last year and her this year and then I just hung up and went up to my room, I wouldn't even explain to my mother, boy some Christmas that was, I want to tell you . . . I don't know, what do you think I should have done? I mean, I saw him a couple of times after that and once we went for a ride, you know, Sunday afternoon down to Peggy's Cove and just sat there and watched the waves, you know how you do, and he said he still loved me and I said sure, I still loved him, but so what, it was all over, I mean it's never the same, is it, I mean it starts out being great and you trust each other and so there's a bit of fooling around, you expect that, everyone's human, right, but there are limits and when you cross that line things can never be the same again, I mean I admit I was really tempted for a while, you know, you remember all the good times, but I said no, it just couldn't be, you have to stand up for yourself, right? I mean, I said, look, Jackie, if I give in on this then that would only be the beginning, let's not kid ourselves. I mean, you have to stand up for yourself, I said, I'm no doormat, I mean it, because if you let someone walk over you once then they'll always walk over you, so you might as well put your mind to it right now, game over mister, I have no intention of being a doormat for the rest of my life, Jackie, so let's not pretend. I mean, you have to learn to hold your head up, right, and if you can't hold your head up, what have you got? Nothing, that's what you've got. A fat lot of nothing. Right?''

"Right,'' said Paleologue, because he understood and agreed and his heart ached for her.

Gould and Rachel loved each other but they didn't have to talk it over quite so much. They knew from the moment they met that they would get married. As is always the case, the soul recognized things the mind refused to see.

"She's really intelligent,'' he explained to the others in the tavern.

"With a body like Rachel's,'' sneered Naseby, "who gives a sweet fuck about her mind?''

"Shut up, Naseby. No, I mean, she's no genius or anything, but . . . well, the other day we were talking about. . . .''
What he meant was that she did have a lush body and she could dance and she was fun to be with but that she was just a little less intelligent than he was, so he knew he could control her and that seemed to him a fine bargain for a marriage. His soul saw that they came from similar economic, social, religious and family backgrounds and would have a great variety of beliefs and prejudices in common. His soul also saw that she was not promiscuous, was not a spendthrift, would not be overly ambitious for her husband, would not nag him if he did not become dean of arts at thirty-three.

"A really great girl,'' he concluded.

And of course Rachel's soul saw that despite Gould's silliness, he was basically a sensible fellow who could keep a job and pay the bills and keep off the booze and stay away from other women and that, though he would never be rich or famous, he would progress up through the English department at a perfectly satisfactory rate.

That was what their souls understood from the first. But in their minds, in that part of them that carried on the routine thinking of life, they had many disagreements.

"Well, if this bitch Francesca is so bloody lovely, what the hell are you doing with your paw in my bra?"

"Jesus, Rachel, I was just saying she was lovely, but . . . ."

"A dream walking was what you said."

"Yeah, all right, but what I mean is, she's . . . unreal, like a vision, and that I'd much rather be here with you because you are real, I mean, this bit of you just here, now . . . ."

"What you mean is that I let you paw me and she doesn't even know you exist, you hypocrite."

"Aw, come on Rachel, you know perfectly well what I meant, you're just twisting what I said . . . ."

"And you're twisting my straps, this one cost me five bucks, so you can just take your meat hooks out of there, I'm going home."

"Aw Jesus, Rachel!"

"Well, are you going to start the car or do I get out and walk?"

"Oh start the car yourself . . . no, not that way, you dumb broad, it has to be in park . . . ."

The next day in the tavern he said to Paleologue, "That Lucy you're going with, she's a really nice kid, eh?"

Paleologue nodded and smiled, waiting to hear what this was about, guessing.

"Yeah, real down-to-earth girl, straight-forward, no frills, no nonsense, I can see the attraction . . . ."

"I can too," said Naseby, "but she's so skinny I expect it's all padding. Am I right?"

Paleologue smiled. "Do you suppose Francesca is in fact a real down-to-earth girl, straight-forward, no frills, no nonsense?"

"What the hell is all this bullshit speculation?" from Ti-Paulo. "If you want to know about the broad why don't you go and fucking ask her? I've never seen such a crew of . . . ."

"How the hell can we? No one knows her, no one even knows anyone else who knows her, hell, we can't even get near her."

"Invite her to your party Friday, shit . . . all she can do is say no."

18

"Invite her to my party? Rachel would kill me, for fuck sake."

And then from mousey little Grilse: "I've already invited her."

Shocked silence. Splutterings of disbelief. Requests for substantiation.

"I told you. I invited her. She'll come. Francesca always keeps a promise. She's that kind of woman."

Pandemonium.

It came out gradually, as things did with Grilse. He'd run into her in the library stacks ("Ran right into her? Are her attractions padded?") and they had smiled at one another. So he had said, "There's a party this weekend, if you like parties, I guess it's your first year here, so if you wanted to meet some people . . . ."

"Thank you, I'd love to."

To the others he said: "I figured she must be a person like everyone else and perhaps being so beautiful maybe she was lonely . . . I guess perhaps she was . . . ."

And in her own way, Francesca was a lonely person. Her beauty, grace, elegance was of that sort that is at the very limit of our experience. When Francesca walked down the street, truck drivers and construction workers were silent, gawking. One did not whistle at Francesca. One did not wink at her or speak to her or yell, "Hey babe, whatcha doing tonight?" One gawked and stood aside to let her pass. So she was lonely.

But once Grilse had broken the ice, everyone found her quite approachable. She did come to the party and she drank beer like everyone else. Nothing makes a goddess human like seeing her tipping back a bottle of beer. She danced with everyone who asked her, listened to everyone's stories and jokes and laughed in all the right places. Ti-Paulo, the group's hardest, most experienced judge of women gave her a brief examination and handed down his opinion to Gould and Paleologue: "Yup. A real down-to-earth girl, straight-forward, no frills, no nonsense. And dumb as they come."

"But she's in science. I heard she gets good marks on her tests."

"I don't mark her tests, I just dance with her."

"But . . . ."

"You get good marks on your essays don't you?"

"Fuck off. No, that physics 104 is a rough course."

Ti-Paulo shrugged.

"Try her. Talk to her. She reacts the right way, but she's not listening to you, she's reading your gestures and tones and guessing the correct responses."

Of course he was right. Rachel talked to her about clothes ("She's got Pucci cleaning rags, for God's sake!"); Ti-Paulo talked to her about painting ("Well, it took four hours, but I think she can now tell a Rembrandt from a Renoir. I think."); Naseby showed her his pornography ("Either she's completely unshockable or she thinks Danish girls have beards."); and Paleologue talked to her of love.

"Nothing matters but love," she said to him one afternoon. It was a warmish day in February and they were standing on a cliff overlooking the sea. "Everyone knows that."

"Yes."

"Poetry is all about love, isn't it?"

"Yes."

"Well, so is science . . . and philosophy . . . and everything . . . the waves there, the waves are in love with the wind and with the rocks."

"Yes."

"It's so simple, really."

"Yes," said Paleologue, "it is simple."

So Francesca became one of the gang and people were not afraid of her anymore. But no one found out whether her father was a Venezuelan oil man or a Russian prince or an Italian ambassador. Somehow it didn't seem to matter: Francesca was just Francesca, she was there, like weather and exams and love. Perhaps Grilse found out things about her, but what Grilse knew was his secret. She called him by his Christian name, John, and when someone had a party she arrived with him and went home with him. Perhaps they spoke of serious things in private, but they were never overheard saying anything but banalities.

"That's a nice piece of music."

"Yes, isn't it."

"The sort of thing that makes you want to dance."

"Oh, would you like to dance?"

"Why, yes, that would be nice."

And later:

"Well, the party seems to be winding down."

"Yes, it does seem to be."

"Perhaps . . . ."

"I suppose we might as well."

"Yes, your physics 104 is on Monday."

"Tuesday, actually, but I should study tomorrow."

"Then I'll get our coats . . . ."

"Yes, please."

They would leave, Grilse with his hands in his pockets, walking on the outside with his head down and Francesca with her hands in her pockets several feet away on the inside, her head up, strolling beneath the streetlights back to the residence. They were together, but they weren't a couple.

The great surprise to everyone was that Francesca's best friend was Lucy. It began as a musical friendship. All the others were listening to Bach and Telemann and Mozart. Francesca had an enormous collection of Chopin and Wagner, while Lucy knew the words to every country and western hit since Hank Williams. Tammy Wynette's "Stand by your Man" expressed perfectly her feelings about life. She had worn out three copies of the single.

They did not meet until some time after Francesca became one of the group, for Lucy had to work days and couldn't stay up late and didn't much like just drinking away her evenings in a tavern and in fact felt uncomfortable with intellectuals like Gould and Ti-Paulo. But there came a Friday night when they were all together in the tavern.

"Hey, old Paleologue!"

"Hey, Lucy-babe!"

"Decided to mix with the workers, eh?"

"Perhaps we should make them sit at another table for a while, think they can ignore us for months and then just come waltzing in here . . . ."

"Gotta pay their dues . . . ."

They would have made a game of it but for Francesca who

21

knew they would sit down and couldn't see the point of teasing them.

"Here's a chair," to Lucy, who replied, "Thanks, boy, what a bunch of nuts they are, if you didn't know better you'd think they all hated each other, the way they tease, no, I'll just leave my coat, have to go to the little girl's room . . . ."

And stop off at the juke box on the way back to push E6 three times for "Stand by your Man."

"I guess there aren't any gentlemen around here, so we have to do our own introductions. I'm Lucy."

"Francesca. How do you do."

"Fine. Yeah, I saw you at a party at Gould's quite a while ago, but, you know how it is, you never get around to saying hello and how's your uncle Bob and all."

"No."

"Gee, I'm so jealous of you for your name. When lover boy here told me you were called Francesca I could have strangled my parents, Francesca is such a pretty name and . . . wait, here it comes . . . ."

And she sang the words of the chorus:

> Stand by your man,
> Give him two arms to cling to
> And something warm to come to
> When nights are cold and lonely.
>
> Stand by your man
> And show the world you love him
> Keep giving all the love you can:
> Stand by your man.

"Oooh, that just knocks me out, it's so great, I mean, I just play it over and over again. In fact, well, I'm almost embarrassed to tell you, but the last thing I do before I go to bed at night, I play it and then when I get into bed I can hear it inside my head. It's like when you were small and you'd say your prayers, well I don't say my prayers anymore, so that's sort of like praying, you know?"

Two days later, on Sunday afternoon, Lucy went to visit

Francesca in her room in residence. Had she been visiting anyone else it might have been a disaster, and in fact there were raised eyebrows and a few snickers from three girls on the front steps. But Francesca was waiting in the lobby in a grey Yves St. Laurent lounging suit and there were no more raised eyebrows or snickers.

"Gee, some place, it's more like a bank than . . . ."

"It's different upstairs."

Girls in curlers, with tattered bathrobes, wearing jeans, sneakers, grubby slippers, the rooms messy, clothes everywhere, hoots and screams and laughter, complaints splitting the air:

"Shut up, for Christ's sake, some people have to work, you know."

"Yeah, deBellefeuille, go get laid or something so we can have a bit of peace."

"If I ever left there wouldn't be a decent piece in this whole stinking place."

"Yahhh!"

"Oh get stuffed, you two."

Lucy was shocked. "I mean I know Rachel is a bit of a garbage mouth, but I thought college girls were . . . supposed to be lady-like, you know."

"In their own way, they are."

But when Francesca closed her door, the sound stopped.

"I put up cork tiles on the walls when I moved in. They don't stop all the noise, but they help a bit."

"Wow! . . . It's like in a magazine . . . ohh . . . gee, and they let you bring all your own furniture and everything?"

"It needed some argument."

"Gee, that's teak, isn't it . . . oh, and velvet curtains, I haven't seen velvet curtains since . . . ."

And while Lucy gazed about, Francesca turned on the stereo and began playing an LP of Tammy Wynette's greatest hits.

"You didn't tell me, and me going on and on the other night."

"I bought it yesterday."

"Mmmm, and the sound, that's really great, I bet it must have cost a small fortune, no, don't tell me, I don't want to know

23

". . . what does AR stand for? . . . "

When they had played Tammy Wynette, Francesca put on a Deutsche Grammophon record of Chopin's greatest hits.

"Ohh, it's really nice, I'm not usually one for long hair stuff, but it's so lovely, what's that one called?"

"The 'Tristesse Etude.'"

"Boy, I've got to get that record, that's really nice."

Then Francesca played the "Prelude" and "Liebestod" from *Tristan and Isolde* and Lucy loved that too.

"And the clothes she has," Lucy told Paleologue later. "I suppose you know since you see her all the time, but I bet you don't know how good they are. Boy, the labels are all Paris, Rome, London, and you should see the stitching, you couldn't get stitching like that around here, not even if you did it yourself . . . and the shoes, one pair must cost as much as all mine together. . . . But, you know, it's funny, she has all these expensive things, clothes and furniture and her stereo and it doesn't make any difference to her at all, she's just like anyone else, you know, we talked about . . . well, things, I can't tell you, just, we talked and . . . ."

They had talked about love and it seemed they had precisely the same ideas about it, whether expressed by Tammy Wynette or Chopin or Wagner. Lucy had told Francesca about her engagement and what it was like trying keep some sort of self-respect in a little place where five out of twenty girls in grade eight had to leave school because they were pregnant.

"I mean, if you really truly love a guy, then I figure it's okay, you know, but in a little place like that, boy, once you get a reputation, that's it, game over . . . ."

"It's the same everywhere."

And Francesca told Lucy things about herself that she had told no one else; Lucy cried and promised never to tell and she kept that promise. She could have given Paleologue a summary: "Francesca has got to be the loneliest person I have ever met, bar none." But she did not even say that.

"If only I could find a man for her. . . . " But as they sat in Lucy's little flat the next Sunday afternoon, she looked at Francesca in her expensive clothes, moving her graceful hands in graceful curves as she talked in her silken, graceful voice and she knew she could not help. "I mean, people have to be

24

right for each other, like Gould and Rachel, or . . . well, I mean, who do I know that I can introduce her to? Take her home and get her a date with Jackie? Sure, he could take her over to the dancehall in Duck Lake and they could sit out back and neck and drink a mickey of rum, she'd really go for that."

"Someone will turn up," replied Paleologue.

"Yeah, like some creepy-crawly under a log, that's what."

"No . . . ."

But to Paleologue's surprise, to everyone's surprise, Dimitri turned up a few months later.

A Saturday in late June, lemon sun in a lemon haze of sky, white curve of beach, empty but for the distant figures of Paleologue, Lucy, Francesca, the three alone in that immensity. They move languidly, one or another going for a dip now and then, a laugh, a cry drifting down the curve, then back to the blankets and silence again. A perfect day.

By and by, just catching the breath of air above the ocean, a sailing yacht slides around the point and into the bay. Off the beach the sails come down, the anchor drops, the dinghy is pulled in. A man climbs down into it and begins pulling for the beach. The first the three know of him is a shadow falling across their legs.

"Oh!".

"Excuse me, I . . . " and he gestures toward the ship. "It's almost dinner time . . . would you care to . . . it would be my pleasure . . . ."

He had been scuba diving further on down the coast and had caught some lobster. It was illegal and he wanted to eat them at once, for to be caught meant confiscation of the diving gear and the yacht. And seeing three people on the beach he had decided . . . it was irregular, he realized, but. . . .

"Oh yes," said Lucy, "Let's go, I just love lobster."

"My name is Dimitri," said the stranger with a little bow. They introduced themselves and began picking up their things. On the way out and while touring the ship they learned something of Dimitri: he was obviously rich, he was alone, he had sailed by himself all the way from the Bahamas, he was polite, gentle and generous. He was also in a desolation of loneliness even worse than Francesca's. "That's why I said we ought to take up his invitation," Lucy told Paleologue later,

25

"Right from the start I could see, I could just see . . . ."

Passing through the saloon he touched a button on the tape machine and the sound of Chopin's "Tristesse Etude" filled the room.

"Ohhh, Francesca . . . ."

"Yes . . . ."

"Hey, look, he's got the same kind of stereo as you do," pointing to the AR on the speakers and the receiver.

"Except for the tape deck. They don't make a tape deck."

"But records aren't much use on a ship."

"No. And music is."

The meal was simple and splendid, heaps of lobster with homemade bread and homemade mayonnaise and green salad and strawberries bought in a little fishing village that morning. Rhine wine.

Ten o'clock came and Lucy said it was a long drive home, she needed her beauty sleep so everyone went up on deck laughing and saying silly things while Dimitri climbed down into the dinghy. He reached up to help Lucy and then Paleologue. It was not until he was untying the painter that Lucy understood.

"Francesca, aren't you . . . ."

"No, I think I'll stay a while."

"Oh . . . well . . . ohh . . . ."

And she had to climb back up to embrace Francesca and cry a little and embrace her again and look into her eyes.

"Oh, Francesca . . . ."

Francesca kissed her on the forehead and whispered something to her.

"You're sure you're going to be all right?"

"Yes."

"Well . . . ."

And they kissed and embraced again and at last Lucy went.

Back on the beach Dimitri shook Paleologue's hand. "We'll be in port on Tuesday."

"We'll come to see you."

Lucy had recovered. "You . . . ." she began pugnaciously, but stopped when she saw the politeness, the gentleness, the generosity in Dimitri's face. He bent down and kissed her on the forehead.

"Yes, Lucy, I'll take care of her. Don't worry."

"Ohhh . . . ."

And when they were halfway along the beach they stopped and looked back at the white sailboat under the full moon ("It would be a full moon," said Paleologue.) and heard the melody of Chopin's Polonaise in A flat major, faintly over the water, under the moon.

Paleologue nodded.

"Perfect."

It was a sensation, of course. Everyone wanted to know what he looked like, where he came from, how he had managed it. Only Grilse remained silent, as always.

"Christ Jesus," Naseby complained. "All she had to do was say the word and I would have crawled through an acre of shit to kiss her ass, and this dude turns up with his . . . ."

"Shut up, Naseby. What I don't understand," said Gould, "is when he put the proposition to her. I mean, if what you say is true, then they weren't alone together for a second. Are you sure they . . . ."

"Not for a second."

"I think they knew each other before," Rachel declared. "Things like that don't just happen right out of the blue. It must have been arranged."

"Lucy says it couldn't have been."

"How would she know?"

"She knows Francesca."

"Yeah, well . . . I still think . . ." because as everyone knew, Lucy was a dummy. She listened to country and western music.

Because they were baffled, they were enraged, an impotent rage as Naseby's final remark indicated: "Well, we can get him to tell us if she fucks as good as she looks."

Gould didn't even bother lifting his gaze from the beer glass as he said, rather sadly, with an air of detached and morose contemplation:

"Shut up, Naseby."

On Tuesday evening they all went down to the dock at the yacht club to investigate. "We'll just see how idyllic this little

27

affair seems after a few days of doing the dishes," said Rachel.

"Huh. If they're there at all. Which I doubt."

"He probably wasn't able to get it up for her. These Adonis types are all fags, you know."

"Shut up, Naseby."

"Eat shit."

"Make them stop, please." Lucy had lost five pounds and had obviously been crying for two days. Whispering: "What if Gould is right? What if they aren't there? What do we do then, call the police or something? Are you sure it was this yacht club and not . . . there they are! There they are! Francesca! Francesca!" and she was running, teetering on her high heels down the wharf to where Dimitri and Francesca were looping lines over bollards.

"Francesca!!"

"Lucy!"

"Francesca, are you. . . ." But one look was enough: Francesca was happy beyond imagining. Lucy looked at her as at a stranger, blinking, her head shaking. Then they embraced and kissed and Dimitri came over and kissed Lucy and shook hands with Paleologue and they went through the introductions and everyone was as awed as Lucy. They were in the presence of perfection.

"They're a couple already," Rachel whispered. "It's as if they'd been together for years."

For they had that intimacy which hangs in the air between husband and wife even when they are at opposite ends of a crowded room. The sense of this accomplished union relaxed everyone at once, and indeed they were all able to accept Dimitri as they had accepted Francesca. The bar was open, the FM playing and everyone talking and wandering around examining the ship. Dimitri showed Grilse and Ti-Paulo how the elaborate sail-raising and trimming mechanisms worked, Gould read labels in the wine cabinet and pronounced the selection "quite adequate," while Rachel advised Francesca about suntan lotions. Even Naseby was moved: after walking about for half an hour with an expensive wrist chronometer in his pocket he dolefully returned it to its drawer in Dimitri's cabin. "Get it next time," he muttered. He did too.

As he was walking up the hill later with Paleologue and

Lucy, Ti-Paulo said: "You know, I had a date to screw a little pig from my still life class, but I don't think I'll bother. I think I'll just go home, have a shower, put on some Chopin and go to bed."

"Yes."

"Feeling sort of . . . grubby, somehow."

"Yes."

"Men," said Lucy, and sighed wistfully.

The lemonade summer poured around them; and their days and nights were days and nights of beaches, endless beaches of curves into endless spirals of white sand, foam-edged on the inside of the curve, spirals up into the lemon sky. It was a summer of friendship and love, lost afternoons on Dimitri's yacht–Dimitri and Francesca's yacht–salt water and sun, and, after a shower, velvet evenings on deck with the AR equipment playing not just Chopin, but Bach, for even the perfect lovers found Glenn Gould relaxing.

That was how they had come to think of Dimitri and Francesca: the perfect lovers. And they shared that perfection, drank it in as they drank in the sun and the endless jugs of lemonade that Francesca and Lucy brought out from the galley.

But August came and the August gales and they could not go out on the yacht anymore. So they went back to the tavern most nights, back to their imperfect selves. They recalled that Francesca wasn't really very bright; that Dimitri was a pleasant fellow, but he didn't seem very bright either. Gould, catching the prevailing mood, delivered a half hour attack on Chopin. Naseby bragged of having filched a dozen pairs of soiled panties from Francesca's laundry hamper.

Through it all Lucy became more and more quiet.

"Hey, Lucy, let's go to a movie tonight."

"Sure, if you want."

"Would you rather stay home and watch TV?"

"No."

"Well, what do you want to see?"

A shrug. "Doesn't matter."

That week he sold his first poem, to a little journal. So he took her to the best restaurant in town to celebrate the sale of

29

the poem and to propose marriage. It was an evening of swish and glitter and lilt, dancing the waltz, lilting, the silver and crystal glittering, Lucy's eyes glittering. Lucy's eyes.

Paleologue swirled the cognac in his glass and looked into her eyes and began: "Lucy, I . . . ."

"No, don't say it," the glitter on her cheeks now, it would never work, it had to end, to end now, she wanted him to take her home now, she was sorry, she was really, really sorry, love, it wouldn't work, they came from two different worlds, love, he was a poet, he had sold a poem, he was going to be famous, he should marry someone from his own world, she was only a dumb typist, no, let's be honest with each other, we always have been, love, we just come from two different worlds, a couple should come from one world, like Gould and Rachel or Dimitri and Francesca, and I'll always love you, always, the glittering tears on her cheeks . . . .

In the dim light outside her flat she fumbles for the key, the tears running down her cheeks, mascara stains on her cheeks, fumbling about until he has to take the purse from her to get the key out, the purse with the sequins on it.

A kiss good-night, good-bye oh my pale Lucy, pale Lucia, light and airy, brave love, from the doorway she lifts her head and gazes into my eyes:

"Think of me now and then."

And closes the door.

Pale Lucy, light and airy and not very bright, she was brighter and braver than I. She could . . . .

She could make you happy.

She could break your heart.

She could . . . .

To hell with you all.

I will not perform for them any longer.

I want only to sleep. I am so tired. I will sleep. I will sleep in the harbour. The ocean is too far away. I will sleep in the harbour. I will not perform for them any longer.

Not for them.

Not for you.

2

Nora Noon

Nora Noon sleeps a lot. Her roommate Lucy doesn't like this and tells her to get out and get a job. "Do something. Find a man." This was some time ago. Nora has a film over her eyes and her fingers seem swollen; she can't get her ring on. Nora gets up in the afternoon and goes out, just out.

"Nora, you're not a bright girl, but you've got looks," her mother used to say. "You shouldn't be moping around. Where's that nice young Grilse fellow you used to go around with?"

"Momma, it's my period."

But that never worked. She got herself a room in the city and Grilse came and took her out some. They were young then and she laughed occasionally. But it's hard for a pretty girl to keep laughing with mended old clothes and cheap new ones. She got jobs. On days off she went out a lot. After a while Lucy came to the city and they got a place together. Lucy was a dummy but she was always happy and her cheap clothes looked happy. Nora tried on some of Lucy's clothes but they looked grey and sad.

Nora Noon wanted more than anything to sleep. She explained to one of Lucy's boy friends, the one with the funny name: "Maybe what's easiest is what's best."

She meant that life was a sort of game and you could take your ball or your skipping rope and go home, but that didn't seem like much of an answer. And if you can't skip rope, you might as well sleep. Paleologue understood.

Then Naseby got wind of her.

"Grab the grey ones when you have the chance," he said. "You can do anything with them and it's a bit of colour in their lives. Nora Noon, here I come."

Naseby treated her like dirt. He also treated her as his slave and fetish creature. With money he had embezzled from Dimitri he bought kinky clothes for her, vinyl waist cinchers with six garters, bras with holes for the nipples and such like.

"Well, gee," Lucy said, "I know they're odd and all, but it's always nice to have clothes. And if it pleases a man there must be something good about it."

Naseby took the precaution always to be nice to Lucy. If there was one thing he understood, it was power, though not so well as Gould's brother Milton and Rachel's sister Mildred. Even in their mid-teens they were into the fetish clothes act, but flagrantly, with rubber and leather. Milton started wearing velvet codpieces with gold thread embroidery. This was after their return and the birth of their child, Mastodon.

Mastodon was a prodigiously stupid kid, hairy and with long teeth. Unlike his parents. Milton had grown up into a strikingly handsome Adonis type, while Mildred was your travelling salesman's dream. They considered themselves *übermenschen*. When Mastodon's characteristics became too obvious to ignore, they were incensed.

"F' Crissake," said Milton, "you woulda thought we could do bettern that."

"So much for fucking genetics."

In any case, neither gave a sweet damn for Nora Noon.

What bothered Nora most were the figures in the cave. They were robed in black, three of them, and they carried candles which threw shadows around her mind. She wanted to know what they were about and she didn't think she'd find out on her own. Nora was not much for thinking, the way people mean thinking, but things went on behind her eyes.

"To Nora," said Paleologue, "the sky is brown and music is noise."

Exactly! But she wasn't crazy; the sky was always brown and music was always noise, even when Naseby got her as worked up as she ever got. This was all tied up in a ball with her second attraction, the first being that she was pretty. She couldn't see blue skies because her metabolism was too low to let her see high frequency colours. Since she could only see brown skies she could never get very excited about anything and couldn't understand why other people did either. This was attractive to men because when they felt the weight of the world on their shoulders, had been jilted or had a hangover, it seemed to them that Nora Noon understood exactly how they felt.

"There are times," said Gould one morning with a thick voice, "when the real answer looks like settling down with Nora and staring at blank walls for the rest of your life." He was quoting Paleologue who had said it much better.

It seemed to men that if they could just make Nora love she might love as she lived. Languid. Long, long kisses, whole nights to make love once. If you could just harness that torpor . . . .

"I'll harness her all right," sneered Naseby as he went off to buy the merry widow with the six garters. For the next while Naseby did a lot more snickering that usual.

At school they used to call her Notty Midnight. She had nothing going for her but that she would put out on the first date and didn't complain. She hung around with a bunch who hung around the lunch counter. "What do you think of the new history teacher, Notty?" "Gee, uhh, he's okay, I guess. . . ." She had a pretty smile and clothes that were easy to undo. Everyone thought she was a real loser except Grilse who was sure there was something, there had to be something. He took her out for a while but all he found was gentleness. She spoke softly, laughed softly and never had harsh opinions about anyone. Once when he was on the front step with her he called her Notty. She burst into tears and cried "You bastard," and slammed the door even though her mother was certainly asleep. But a week later she saw him at a dance and smiled at him. He took her home that night but he resented her. After a while he stopped going with her and didn't see her again until she looked him up in the city.

Naseby did two things for Nora. The first was to get Grilse drunk and find out about her nickname. This betrayal caused Grilse no end of agony; he couldn't decide between killing himself or Nora. The second thing Naseby did was show that Nora had an aura.

"Poignant prurience," said Paleologue. "Naseby brings things out in people, the scamp."

Naseby took Nora to a party at Gould and Rachel's. She was wearing a plain grey dress and no one much noticed her until Naseby began whispering about what Nora wasn't wearing underneath it. Grilse managed to get her aside and ask her about it.

"What is he doing to you, Nora?"

A shrug.

"I'm worried about you. Naseby is . . . ."

"I know."

"I'm sorry I told him about your nickname. I was drunk and he kept at me . . . ."

Then, in whispered desperation: "Why don't you just leave me alone?"

That same desperation Grilse had seen the night he called her Notty Midnight. No one else had ever seen it. Grilse was terrified in that moment that he would marry her. He felt responsible.

Nora turns and goes back to the party; Grilse stays on with the coats, tears in his eyes, beating the wall slowly, softly, quietly.

But the idea of poignant prurience caught on. The men were reading porn and talking to the girls, with a touch of bravado, about their bras. Gould tried to get Rachel to wear a few things, but she went tough on him and started talking women's lib. Gould figured he might edge her into the anti-bra lib but all she did was spend a fortune on tailored slacks and plain white blouses. She had her hair cut short.

Milton and Mildred had a chuckle when they next saw her and heard her blatherings. "Look, sis," said Milton with a canny pretence of sincerity, "if you're going for this anti-man stuff, you ought to do a proper job of it, really explore it, you know?"

"You're accusing me of insincerity."

"No, no, let me explain . . . ."

The burden of his argument was that she ought to have an affair with Nora. It took a few hours, but his calm concerned tone, along with his utter dishonesty in argument and Rachel's stupidity, brought her around. That evening she called Nora and asked her if she'd like to go shopping with her.

"They have a sale on slacks at . . . ."

Nora protested that she didn't have any money but Rachel said she could window-shop. Nora was always a bit slow with lies, so she gave in. At two the next afternoon she was waiting in front of the hotel where the tavern was where all the men were sitting and talking about Nora's grey dress and what she wasn't wearing underneath it just fifty feet away unknown to them. Rachel came ten minutes late. She tried being affectionate, then tried treating her like dirt like Naseby but only succeeded in being patronizing.

"What a pretty grey dress," she cooed.

"Uhh, gee, thanks."

"Of course, I've given up dresses entirely. I refuse to be the brainless sex-toy of the hairy-chested chauvinists and I'm thinking, in fact, of forming a group . . . ."

The group had its first meeting that afternoon in Nora's flat. Rachel had bought her a pair of panties with a split crotch and wanted to see them on. This led to Nora showing her kinky silks and leathers and both of them trying them on which in turn led to the bed and a rather maladroit bout of lesbian intercourse. Rachel went home a newer, stronger woman and taunted Gould with her success. "And she wears the nicest tasting lipstick on her nipples . . . ."

Gould was horrified, furious.

"What about me?" he raged. "Don't you suppose I have feelings? Marriage is a two-way thing, you know. You could at least have let me watch . . . ."

A whole new world was opening up for the young couple.

The figures in the cave stayed away for a while after Nora's incident with Rachel. It was not that sexual intercourse was new to her—she had been getting banged pretty regularly since she was thirteen—but now she began to sense the musk, the hum about her that others sensed. Men at parties stared at her, peeked at her, coughed and stammered when trying to speak to her. The women despised her. But she could also feel it in her body. Naseby grew dissatisfied with just the kinky clothes; he made her shave her pubic hair then forbid her to wear panties, so that she was unable to ignore her sexuality even walking to the corner to buy cigarettes or a jar of instant coffee. What had been hidden, ignored, much like any other woman's was now naked and rouged, defenceless against breezes and crossed legs. Nora was in a hot blush all the time, her eyes bright and active, ashamed of what everyone must know (did know, if Naseby could help it) yet fascinated by it all. Naseby had been right, Nora liked being noticed, and if what made people notice her was a bit questionable then that added spice to it.

But the figures in the cave returned. They came even more than before and stayed longer. They came in her dreams and when she was trying to sleep wondering if Lucy lying next to her would go for the same thing as Rachel because surely it would be better with someone you liked (she would and it was) and in the morning when she was half awake trying to think of a reason for getting up and even in the afternoons lying on the bed in the black vinyl waist cincher with the six garters and the smoke grey nylons according to Naseby's instructions, waiting for him and touching herself and wondering why she was in this cave and what the three men in the hooded black gowns wanted of her. She had been afraid of them when they first came to her as a little girl but she got used to them over the years. After she finished school she tried reading books on the interpretation of dreams but they didn't help; but they got her on to psychology books generally and she continued to read them. She was reading one that afternoon and not understanding, seeing just words as she waited for Naseby and touched herself and glanced every now and then at the figures to see what they were doing now, but all they were doing was standing there the same as they always did except to come and go. Then the door was flung open and Gould came raging in throwing his arms about and tearing his hair and ranting on about something or other. Nora figured it had to do with her and Rachel making love, that was obvious fairly early on, so she didn't bother listening. She never bothered to listen much to anyone because it seemed to her that people usually talked to themselves. She also thought that people didn't listen much either which was why she didn't bother talking much. People were just there, like the figures in the cave.

The figures in the cave seemed to have some secret and that was why they interested her more than herself or other people. With all the noise Gould was making she couldn't read so she laid the book aside and watched to see what the figures would do. Surely there would be some reaction? Obviously they were part of her mind and perhaps that was it: she wasn't reacting either. Oh well. It seemed nothing could move them. This was confirmed when Gould raped her. He hurt her quite a bit but she kept wiping the tears from her eyes so she could watch the figures. They did nothing.

Gould lay on top of her. He was crying too. Between the sobs he uttered words: "Guilt . . . repentance . . . punishment . . . atonement. . . . " Nora couldn't help hearing.

"Perhaps you should go now," she said at last. He was heavy on her.

Gould stood up and stared at the floor for a while. Suddenly he jerked his head up and glared at her.

"Bitch!" he cried. "Bitch! Circe!"

He turned and bolted out the door waving his arms as he went. Nora lay there much as she had with her book. The figures just stood watching. Presently she got up and used a deodorant douche. She powdered, reapplied her lipstick. Lying on the bed again she was ready for Naseby whenever he should decide to come. She picked up the book again but the words were only words and she let it slip to the floor. Lucy had a date right after work and wouldn't be home until at least midnight. There was nothing to do but look at the figures and wait for Naseby and wonder how long it would be before Gould realized his fly was down.

But she had no idea when Naseby would show up, she couldn't know about Gould and his fly and the figures turned and glided away, the medium-sized one first, the fat one second and the tall sepulchral one last. So Nora had nothing to do but stare at the ceiling and cry quietly as the room grew darker.

It couldn't go on forever. Naseby put her through her paces like a trained dog, but she could sense that he was losing interest. The rich purple throb of her aura became a pale blue hum. The men let their women go back to their white cotton bras. People could speak to her without stammering, and the things they said weren't all that pleasant. She went to a last party where she was jostled and tweaked now and then, but the interest of the evening was elsewhere. Gould was telling about his time in jail for indecent exposure; Rachel, wearing a flowery, flouncy dress, was showing off her new wig and telling people they were the coming thing. Nora stood alone in a corner without even the smirking attentions of Naseby who had said he would come later. When he did arrive it was in the company of the goldilocked boy of twelve dressed in black velvet with lace at the cuffs and a lace jabot below his silky downed chin. Grilse came rushing over to Nora: "There, you see what he's like, the rotten bastard, you see what . . . ."

Nora Noon ran past him to the bedroom where the coats were. Grilse was shocked by her beauty, the frailty of her arms and legs flashing, the hot flash of her aura when the short black skirt fluttered up to reveal the blush of one naked buttock. Then she was gone.

She was gone. Paleologue saw her again years later and then only by accident. He was on a train going to visit Ti-Paulo, the hard-nosed little painter who had had an affair with Rachel and who was now working on a mural for a government department. It was a mid-week trip in January and the train was half empty. Paleologue wrote a poem as he travelled along, a poem of love and travel and when he got home he added a last verse that was very short.

He recognized Nora while he was going to the dining car. She sat alone, calm and touching in repose, one definition of woman. This was her true aura, Paleologue saw, this was the prurient poignancy of Nora Noon and it had only a little to do with Notty Midnight. Only a little, but some.

"Nora?"

"Why . . . it's . . . . I never could remember your name."

They chatted a bit and then she agreed to go with him to the dining car. (Rather, thought Paleologue, I go, she goes, we go together.) He noticed, when she took off her glove, that she was wearing a gold wedding ring. The black Persian lamb coat was tailored and stylish and gave her a look of delicacy and confidence that was also part of her definition of woman. She knew who she was and where she was, but she walked like a stranger, hesitant and curious, her eyes bright and open with myopia. Underneath the coat a grey dress and underneath it . . . .

"Yes," she blushed. Paleologue, thinking of the blushing mound Naseby had made them all touch, knowing it blushed now, blushed too. "It became a habit for me," she explained. "I don't think about it often," like the touch of pink through the Ti-Paulo fresco on the ceiling of Paleologue's study, an airy flight of muses in scanty silks, like the rhythm in the poem he had just written, like smoke through an autumn wood . . . .

"And what have you been doing all these years?" he asked.

Nora sits on her haunches in an African village. The children are teaching her jacks. In the morning she taught them writing. Nora plays the game with energy and laughter. She does not have much of their tongue, their twittering ideograms, but she is a happy starling. Down at the edge of the river with the women washing clothes she listens and makes her quizzical smile. They joke all the time and Nora is sure they have something she doesn't. Perhaps she should stay here forever; it is a village with a living economy, good weather, little disease. But after a while her term is up and she goes back home. She knows she was in one of the happiest villages in Africa; that they do have something she doesn't, but that she has to go home to find it.

Imperialism: Nora remembered this word from school. It has something to do with gunboats, those great big ones and phrases like Boxer Rebellion, Balkans, sphere of influence. It happened in the 19th century.

Nora knew Ti-Paulo. She had taken a drawing course from him at an art school. It was Tuesday evening at eight. They had real models and most of the students were women. Ti-Paulo was a good teacher and Nora wasn't much of a draughtsman. When she drew feet they looked like hooves; but she got better. When the course began, Ti-Paulo said:

"I am a serious painter and this is a serious course. I don't give a sweet fuck about your souls or how much you want to express them. Each drawing is a work of art. It is a complex problem of form, tone, composition, line, volume. You will learn to see these problems; you will learn solutions. The more solutions you learn, the better able you will be to express yourself, maybe."

To the model he said:

"Take off."

The model took off her robe.

"Assume a pose."

To the students he said:

"That is a nude woman. You will get something of her and of yourself onto the piece of white paper which is before you. For the next two hours that paper contains your heaven and your hell. You will therefore treat it with due respect, firstly by addressing it properly, so . . . ."

He held out his pencil toward it at arms length and said, "Hello paper."

The students addressed their papers, Ti-Paulo grunted his approval and the course was launched.

Nora learned some drawing from that course. She also learned some Ti-Paulo. He was a real artist, he scraped a living from it. He had a show that winter and the critics took it seriously. Real people bought the pictures. She was terrified of him because he was real, he really did it, because he took her seriously: "Fine, you have a broad with hooves. That's okay. Now what are you going to do with the hooves, what is the problem of the hooves, how do you solve the hooves?" He was a real artist because he worked, he did it. He was a person because he also laughed easily. He laughed at himself.

The more things Nora did, the less she worried about the figures in the cave. The less she worried, the more she wondered about them. It was quite obvious to her that she must not tell people about them, but she was unable to trick herself into the corollary: that everyone else saw something similar and wouldn't tell. Some people, like the alcoholic newsman she lived with, had visions they talked about but it didn't seem quite the same. The newsman, for example, saw snakes the morning after. For Nora, every morning was this morning and it wasn't after anything.

At last she went to a psychiatrist. They got on pretty well. He said, "One hour, this is the time you give me. You can't expect much. But you know that, fine." When she told him about the figures he told her not to worry too much, she had gotten along with them all these years, she could probably keep on. As long as she could manage her life she needn't worry.

This was about what Nora had figured on her own, but she was glad to have it confirmed. She went back to her life.

One night, in the summer of her twenty-ninth year, Nora Noon could not sleep. She slipped out of bed and stood dressing and watching for the least movement from the alcoholic newsman: but he just lay there, his stubbled face contorted in the bitter grin he wore when he dreamt of discovering corruption in public office and then having his editor refuse to publish the story. He just lay there drunk, grinny, snorey, farty, smelly.

She slipped out of the house and walked to a quiet little park where she sat on a bench to watch the east grow light. It was here and then that she met Roger Portable, the man who had forgotten his own name, in the summer of her twenty-ninth year.

Roger Portable was a man of property, in which he lived, and a man of independent means which he spent sparingly on the things he needed to live the life he wanted. He was a scholar. He wrote articles for journals. In the summer of his forty-second year he was in the habit of working through the night and going for a walk in the cool of the dawn. Roger Portable was a man of substance, and when Nora Noon first saw him, his considerable substance was dressed in tweeds of dated and eccentric taste. He laid a pudgy finger against the wart of his pudgy nose and said,

"Oh, excuse me, I . . . ."

"I'm sorry, is this your bench?"

"No, it is the public's bench. I am in the habit of using it at this hour."

"Oh, then it's sort of yours, isn't it?"

"No more than it is yours. But there is room for both of us. I wonder, if I were to sit upon it, would you be so kind as to remain and watch the sun rising with me?"

She smiled and he eased his bulk down some feet away from her.

"Habit," he said, "is comforting to us in a chaotic world. Insomuch as it gives us the illusion of order we have peace. Where there is peace, there can be politeness."

He glanced at her with piggy eyes. She smiled.

"I would guess from your apparent age and manner of dress that you belong to the more bohemian part of our society. Do your people value politeness?"

"Well . . . uhh . . . I guess you could say so. It's different though. They wouldn't want to admit it."

"Quite. Politeness when broadly defined is something I think we all desire. It is one of the finer . . . ."

He went on. He went on about politeness for some time while the sun rose before them, light through the trees, deep, clear light of the sky, deep and clear above a city of mad men, sick men, slaves and thugs, cries of children, torn people, the machinery grinding on as Roger Portable ran on about a world where people were polite to one another until he stopped and swabbed his face with his handkerchief.

"You don't need to be afraid of me," said Nora softly.

"Afraid?"

"People who run on are hunted men."

Roger Portable looked at the bright sky and at Nora and at the ground. "Yes," he said. "I'll go now. Perhaps we will see one another again."

"Perhaps."

They ran into each other every morning for a week. The following week they were married.

"Because you found my bench."

"Because you found me on it."

As good reasons as any, they felt, and a better marriage than most.

Paleologue tried to order them another coffee, but the waiter said they were almost there.

"Already?" said Nora. "And I've spent all this time jabbering about myself. I do apologize."

"On the contrary, I have met very few people who have actually lived in Africa. It was most interesting."

"Now you're teasing me," she laughed.

When he and Ti-Paulo were at last settled at a table in a tavern they talked about Nora.

"Yeah, I remember her."

"You knew her?"

Ti-Paulo explained about the drawing class.

"She didn't have much talent for draughtsmanship, so far as I could see, but she was a good kid. Open mind. There was something about her."

Paleologue talked about her aura.

They were both mildly surprised when she dropped in on them the next day. She chatted, admired Ti-Paulo's work in a way that showed she knew about it, reminisced, blinked her eyes and smiled shyly. While leafing through a book on Henry Moore she came upon a drawing called "Figures in a Cave." She blinked her eyes at it then shrugged her shoulders. As she was leaving, tall and assured in her coat, a little girl in her walk, she turned and smiled her remarkable smile.

"It's funny how time passes," she said.

"You can say that again."

"It's funny how time passes," she said.

3

Break-up:
From the Journals of Ti-Paulo

I am having a vernissage

I am having a vernissage this week, to open my fifth one-man
show. The critics divide a painter's work into periods (blue,
pink, constructionist, etc.). If his shows are rationally spaced
there will be one at the end of each period. What the critics
don't mention (it's none of their goddamn business, either) is
that painting periods are usually life periods. More specifically, woman periods. The work this time is figure drawing,
the woman is Odile Saulara. I'm finished with figure drawing
for a while. I have a feeling about Odile.

There's a muddle of work since September–big, little,
good, bad–and I have to choose twenty-five. I looked them
over today and wished I could leave them all out. I don't enjoy
peddling my work. Cocktail parties. What do they have to do
with the blank canvas? A nice bit of the aesthetic absolute,
that, but the framing and the invitations and the hanging and
the cheap sherry (who can afford cocktails?) mess up the work
for a month on either side. There's always something going
wrong. Last time, I walked into the gallery a week after the
opening and found the floor covered with iron-mongery on
pedestals. Unbelievable. Scrap metal cluttering up my show.

Sculptors are just welders with arrogance. No brain. So I had to tell them to get the junk out or down came my show. How can you stay sane with imbeciles like that attacking you?

Vernissage: French for varnishing. Last century when everything was stinking big oils, the exhibitions would schedule a sort of pre-opening for the painters and hangers-on and the painters would slap on a new coat of varnish to make the garbage look fresh for the public the next day. (Turner completely repainted one of his one time and the judges wanted it disallowed because it was not the thing they'd accepted.) My stuff is drawing under glass. Just for the fun of it, I ought to varnish the whole lot. Hah.

A show is an exhibition of the most painful failures, the ones closest to being successes. The last time Paleologue was here we talked about Shakespeare. He thinks *Hamlet* is his greatest failure, I say *Lear*. We decided we could die happy if just once in our lives we could fail as well as he did regularly twice a year for twenty years.

P. is coming to town the day after tomorrow for the vernissage and will stay the weekend, perhaps next week too. Damn writers for their mobility. P. has some sort of fascination with train trips. I suppose that says something for him. I suppose it says something for the two of us that at our age we can still talk seriously about Shakespeare.

Hope Gussie is coming too. I love that woman, but Odile will be in agonies of jealousy.

Odile, her life and character

Odile Saulara is not her real name. Probably Mary Smith or Betty Grable Jones or something. She was an orphan, never adopted. A couple of foster homes where the wives spent the agency allowance on gin and the husbands molested her. You often find that a thin, beautiful woman was an ugly, nervous kid, all elbows, knees and teeth. Nerves keep the weight down. I should know.

I don't know how she did at school, but it seems clear she had no interest in it whatsoever. Sitting in grade eleven history class chewing her tongue over the weekly test. Chewing her pencil too, no doubt. Women are such pigs, slobs. (Men are much more graceful because of sports. They have to learn to negotiate spaces quickly, avoid objects. Women never do. Line them up with shaved legs and screens above mid-thigh and how do you tell them apart? The women are the ones with the bruises on their legs.) They knew damn all about history either, think all history is between their legs. Well, there are worse ways of looking at it. Anyway, Odile over the history test. Around her, all these strange people. Odile looks at them, into them. One moment she knows she knows them; the next she's in terror at their cockiness, their animal smells. She looks back at the paper: who the fuck was Hildebrand, anyway?

Odile was a model for a few years (fashion, not painting) before she made the move up to editorial work. A lot of people hate her guts (fashion is a filthy world) because she appears sharp and confident. This is no more a lie than such observations usually are. She knows her world and knowledge is power. Power is terror?

Limited knowledge: she doesn't know us, can't figure any of us, not even Gould. Once on the train she ran into a couple of yobbos from down home. They'd come up here for the work, the usual thing, and were going home to get drunk, the usual thing. They insisted on paying for her drinks at those train prices and when the talk fell down they got into a ferocious argument about clouds. Odile thought that was wonderful, "so fresh, so open to new experiences." It took me two hours to make her admit she thought them losers.

Because she doesn't understand us, she fears us. Being with her, I see this better than the others do. But what the hell, somewhere or other in there we're all scared shitless. Henry and Hildebrand are both dead. Their works live after them. Sure.

The thing itself

Well, it was a vernissage all right. Same as all the others except better organized. That is, disgusting. Sold six things at $800. After the gallery's cut that's $2880. With the cost of booze, the party, invitations, framing and income tax, I should clear $1500. It should sell a few more before it's taken down. My Vollard claims he has a couple of Steins and Guggenheims lined up. I wish he'd told me, I could have jacked the prices.

Naseby was there. What a wreck. He's put on weight and was wearing a lot of immense costume jewellery not because he likes it, but because no one else does. Purple bags under his eyes. He's as snide as ever but some of the edge has gone off it. I think he's been beaten a few times. And not just by his girl friends and boy friends.

I was standing by the big blue pastel nude (drawing with colour, getting to painting again by the back door) when he came in. Odile shot me a glance asking if he was okay, so I went over to him. Shifty eyes. I think he'd read every person in the room by the time I got there. Read their sexual preferences and liquid assets, anyway. He gave me a hand that was like a pile of uncooked sausage.

"Hit the big time at last, eh? Heh, heh."

"Yeah, need a loan? For a pack of cigarettes?"

Mutual insults are the only way to get along with Naseby. He was beaming. But Naseby has never been scared of arty people; he thinks we're all frauds and losers. Just that some are amiable losers and some aren't.

"Why don't you visit the crapper before you drop your load in your pants?"

Sharp as ever. Social fusses always play hell with my bowels. He'll pay for it, though. I told him to open his pocket.

"Heh, heh, always fast with the remarks, eh? Who's the long piece of cunt over there. Looks like a clothes horse gone to seed. Nerves shot."

"I don't know, really. Odd, too, since she's been living with me for three years."

"You always had a good eye for skirt, Paulo. Still, if you want to have her taken off your hands . . . ."

"Just call you. Boiler Room Enterprises, isn't it? Featuring Moose Pasture Mining and Exploration?"

"Let you in on the ground floor. Make a killing. Buy a yacht. Live off the interest."

"Free to paint for the rest of my life."

"Insurance for the whole family, college for the kiddies, nice little annuity when you're sixty."

"Count me in."

"You artists have no fucking imagination."

I sloughed him off on Gussie and Paleologue (that's another story) and went to see Odile.

"My God, who is that . . . that . . . ."

"Careful. That's Naseby. Repulsion is his big line, he opens a lot of doors with it."

"Oooo," and an elegant mannequin's shudder, "when he looked at me it was like being handled by some obscene, slimy swamp creature."

Now I've heard this about Naseby before. When women speak of him, the words slime, pus and vomit figure prominently. I'm worried about it. Odile has a strong streak of masochism, self-disgust, and Naseby is the guy to satisfy her. I like her, we've had a good three years together. It's hard to believe people act that way, but I watched her for the rest of the night, and I'm worried. It was like a snake and a rabbit. I brought her a drink one time when she was supposedly listening to the mumblings of Grilse (God only knows where he came from—or went back to. Haven't seen him for ten years; he only stayed half an hour. Weirdo. Loser.), listening to Grilse, but her upper lip was beaded with sweat, eyes glazed, flush on her throat down to her breasts, fingers jumping all over, pecking at her cigarette. Naseby saw all this too, and pretended to ignore it. What he really wanted was to take her out back and whip her in the storage room. I'm very much afraid that's what she wanted too.

A little later he's standing with a bunch of my students from the art college. He grabs one by the boob and squeezes. Giggles and squeals: "It's me, Patsy Painter, in the presence of real evil, tee-hee!" Odile is quivering with jealousy, desire, curiosity. Her nostrils flare like a horse at the starting gate.

This is real trouble. Nothing I can do about it either. Naseby is playing a waiting game, trying to drive her crazy with lust, me just crazy. I don't know about her, but he won't get me.

Going out with P. and G. tonight. That'll be fun. Ho. Ho.

Odile borrowed an item from the office that they'd been photographing and looked as smashing as you'd expect. (Borrowed, hell: she stole it.) Of course, she's four inches taller than me, so I had to stand back while she made her entrances and exits. I sometimes think being short is the central fact of my character. However, I looked pretty snazz myself: she'd bought me a velvet suit and the doings. I like the suit but take it as a bad sign. Women only give presents at beginnings and endings. It'll be funny getting back into jeans and tee shirts when she leaves. Oh yes, she's leaving. Hasn't said so, but the suit gave it away.

P. said it was his favourite restaurant for occasions, but the place was getting to be so full of ghosts for him that he was going to have to change. Gussie won't let him sleep tonight till she finds out about that.

Very pleasant evening for me, but too much going on underneath. Odile, of course. She identified Gussie's dress right off and found it wanting. She ignored me most of the night, cooed at Paleologue who was very polite and chatty with her. He disagreed with things she said but never in a way that said she was stupid. Not that it would matter: he could call her a skinny, vulgar bitch and she'd lap it up. (Me she'd come at with a knife; did, in fact, the night I met her.) Of course it was all phony super-politeness with Gussie who took it very well, I'd say. I can't be bothered with all this what-is-she-really-saying stuff, leave it for the shrinks, but I tried tonight, just to see if Gussie was using the knife back, and she wasn't. It makes sense. Gussie is all of herself, more a person that most of us ever get to be. She has a great marriage and, so far as showbiz is predictable, a great career. Why should she worry about a hysterical sub-editor of a fashion mag? No reason that I can see, and doesn't act as if there were, though Odile began cursing her the moment they left us and is still doing so in the john. I can hear the gnashing teeth from here.

(Interesting possibility: Paleologue offered me their farm for the summer, they're going to be in Europe. Writers are so lucky: how the hell can I use a stone house? The windows are all too small to let in enough light for a painter. Still, the idea attracts. If Odile does go, rather, when she goes, I think I'll get in touch with Dimitri and Francesca. The adorable dimwits spent a fortune last year on a really lovely place near Paleologue's and I know they'll never use it again. A bit of upkeep in exchange for the rent, some swimming to get back into shape, bird watching to soothe the love-torn soul, hmm, yes.)

After 1.P-K4, White's game is in its last throes

If any of my friends caught me being gentle, they'd never let me live it down. The times I've seen people trying to help other people out of pure charity I could count on ten fingers. The times I've seen it work I could count on two. When it comes right down to it you can't really help anyone else (except for a loan, the name of an honest lawyer) and you can't expect anyone to help you. I admit it sounds hard, but to go through life expecting to be helped every time you're in trouble is arrogant, inconsiderate and suicidally stupid.

I'm wandering a bit from Breyer's statement. What I mean is, I'm willing to try something different with Odile and for me gentleness is a Queen pawn opening. I suppose the question arises, though: whose game was in its last throes, hers or mine?

Anyway, this morning before I got out of bed, I decided to try some gentleness. Odile sleeps until eleven on Saturday. I was up and off to the shops by nine thirty, back at ten fifteen getting things ready. At eleven on the dot I woke her with (blush) a kiss.

"What's wrong with you?"

"Shut up and drink your bloody mary," but with a grin. (Smile you bastard, she's never up to much in the mornings.) Gave her the papers, her make-up case (more portable than the pig-sty on her dressing table), a mirror, and arranged the light around her. I gave her a bed bath, all very tender, massage with oil, powder all over. While she finished up on the face, I got the food ready (as copied from my exquisitely lettered menu):

Fresh Strawberries Chilled in White Wine
Eggs on Muffins Baked in Cheddar Sauce
Hot Buttered Toast with Jams and Honey
Thick Sliced Back Bacon
Fried Sliced Green Tomatoes
Champagne
Turkish Coffee
Turkish Cigarettes

And a red rose in a bud vase.

Painters usually go for chubby women no matter what the fashion. What's the use of a woman cluttering up the house if you can't use her for a model? I've used Odile a few times with indifferent results. You can do some interesting things with bones and splayed limbs; adventurous composition is easier. On the whole, though, the chubby ones are more useful.

But when it comes down to living beauty, the real woman, I have to admit I'm a man of my times. I lugged the dishes back to the kitchen and returned to the bedroom and stopped in the doorway: there was something about her that got beyond the flesh. Everything very haute couture, of course, the whole zazz world. Hair in elegant disarray, high cheekbones, wrist bent back. I felt all grubby, privileged to be there. Odile, I realized, was the most beautiful woman I have ever known. I know enough else about her to know she's a mess, but when she's at peace, she's perfection. At that moment I think she believed it all, the whole shooting match, she was one person. I almost cried.

I stopped just outside the door and gawked at her. The curtains were pulled back and the sun streaming in, a fine, fresh, spring sun. The leaves were just bursting on the big maple outside the window and she was gazing toward it (not at it) with her face turned quarterface from me so I could see the good lines in her cheek, her throat. (I don't mean she was doing it on purpose.)

And it all fell on me. Any fool knows the main lines of the argument, can repeat it without effort. But you forget it's real and every now and then it hits you like a post maul: I saw the perfection of her and saw also that it was not for me. Because the whole can of worms was implied in what was visible.

She turned and smiled at me. Rather, she turned and smiled out of some learned habit at the shadow in the doorway. I went over and told her I loved her and she said she adored me. Like the suit: when they talk adoration, it's already too late. We chatted about the papers and this and that and after an hour we made love. Two hours for that. Never better. Never could be.

She went out shopping (she said) about three, so I'm sitting here with a beer looking at the same tree (now more or less in shadow–the sun has gone to the other side of the house) fumbling through these crippled notes (my prose is having one of those days) and hoping she doesn't come back. Perfection would be nice just once in my life.

An incident with my father

He was about fifty then and having his problems. My mother
had finally taken her money and gone to Rome to live among
the gigolos. The old man was hitting the booze, his law practice was slipping. Then he started going with a new typist from
the architect's down the hall. It got serious. He called and
offered me the plane fare home.

They met me at the airport, the old man alternating between blushes and feeling her up while sticking out his chin
at me. He needn't have bothered: I never had much use for
the old lady either. The girl's name was Lucy, quite pretty,
blonde, scatterbrained. She was about my age, mid-twenties
then, knew something of what it was all about. You got the
idea she had been married once, though the old man said later
she hadn't. Had the idea also I'd met her somewhere but
didn't mention it; would have embarrassed all of us. I play
rough but I play nice. She was nice too. A piece of fluff, really,
but with life in her and eyes that looked at you. I approved
but didn't let on to the old man right away.

The house surprised me. It was very subtle, really. The old
man hadn't changed much except the living room and I had
to look hard to see what was gone from there: a few pieces of
ironmongery from the end tables, a couple of French chairs,
all the china and glassware, that is, a cabinet full of Waterford,
about ten vases and candlesticks and a little photo portrait of
herself in a little oval china frame. As I say, I was surprised.
The old man was on his way to recovery. I thought for a while
it might have been Lucy but concluded later it couldn't have
been: she was a dummy, but she'd never have tried that sort
of thing. A dummy with a way with people.

This I discovered from the way she played hostess. She put
out the best tableware for honoured son, was careful with it
but not finicky. Served the meal without apologies (even if she
knew about the old lady's cooking, this showed a cool hand)
and never once called my father by his first name. That last was
genius. I could hardly wait to call her Mommy.

After putting the dishes in the dishwasher she came out and
sat with us a while. Then he called a taxi and sent her home.
Sweet. But I'd had a few and let it pass.

The old man had had a few himself. He is a stupid man with an inclination for sneakiness. In this he always fails with me. He's about as nonchalant as a dog who's just shit on the stairs. That night he was doing his hearty act.

While I was living at home I detested this heartiness. Now I had to suppress the laughter. He was getting drunker and heartier. "Paul, my boy, I know we don't see eye to eye on a lot of things, but we've always been able to talk man to man . . . ." The way he actually said it took five minutes and had fifteen qualifications and fifty ho-hos. "Have another drink, my boy, ho-ho, man to man, straight from the shoulder." I let him go on like this for an hour or so and then put the arm on him for $800 worth of painting. That sobered him up right smart.

He got thoughtful and poured another drink, sticking out his lower lip to show he was looking for a snappy phrase. I let him sweat.

"When you get older son, when there's more of your life past than future . . . ."

He was so impressed by that last bit that he stopped to savour it, wondering if he shouldn't have gone for criminal law after all.

"The decree absolute was granted last week," he said. "After thirty years, it's done."

"Don't get solemn for my sake."

"And don't you get smart with me. Let me tell you something, in thirty years at law I have never seen a divorce to get flip about. Never. They say that marriage is dying, and I suppose it is, but it still has magic for people. Sometimes it's the moon in June, sometimes it's religion, sometimes friends and relatives, but mainly, I think, because of living together. People will get married for any number of reasons, a lot of them bad, mostly in ignorance of what's coming, but let me tell you, there's always hope, always. And when it dies, the ghost of it lives on. To live is to hope, when you're young you have hope. But as each hope is killed or compromised you die a little. A divorce is the end of a very big hope. It isn't the last years you remember, it's the first ones."

Yeah, well, what was I suppose to say? I had a terrible impulse to laugh in his face, bray like a donkey and walk out on him. But then he would claim the sale of the painting was not binding. I was doing well enough but not that well. $800 free of commission and income tax. I kept a straight face, poured some more, lit a smoke. Besides, I was not unmoved by what he said. I'd heard similar things before, but it was well said and, looking back on the three or four divorces I knew about, it seemed fairly accurate. Didn't know the old man had so much blood in him.

"And now . . . ."

"Now you're hoping again."

"Not very hard. I'm not much of a catch however you look at it. If she's a golddigger, she's a damn stupid one. Even with the booze the doctors give me twenty years. No, she's had a hard time, fell pretty hard once, and just wants a home, a man to take care of. I figure I can give her ten years before she wants something more. Then she's free if she wants it."

"And you'll be sixty?"

"Fifty-nine."

A lie.

"Why marry her at all?"

"Live with her?"

We batted that around a while. I figured he was going soft in the head. Having hankerings: he could have been consistent at least. Then he told me.

"I was having supper one night, if you could call it that. Sitting at the kitchen table with greasy dishes all over the place, eating a fried egg with the yolk broken and some hard bread with rancid butter. There were some scraps of hamburger on another plate. All of a sudden the cat is up on the table, after the scraps, see. I keep on eating, the cat keeps on eating, we're watching each other. Suddenly it dawns on me, I'm fifty years old and I'm going to spend the rest of my life eating supper with a cat. Was I? No goddamn fierce I wasn't."

We had a good laugh over that. I expect he'd mouthed it around and knew it was a good story. I poured a last one and took it upstairs with me while the old man shut up the house. Going past his room I heard a noise and realized Lucy hadn't gone home at all. I laughed about that too, but I did it quietly. Even the ludicrous has a touch of the sacred.

Hah!

Naseby was around on the pretext of looking at some pictures, said he wanted to buy something but wanted me to get the gallery's forty per cent. Since he would obviously want to keep it himself, I knew he was lying. So I was mildly curious and invited him to stay for lunch. Lunch for me was some leftover lasagna, and for Naseby it was leftover lasagna with as much castor oil and milk of magnesia as I figured I could sneak into him. Paleologue has always viewed Naseby with amusement; my amusement is in seeing him suffer a bit.

And suffer he did. Gobbled down the whole time bomb then settled back in his chair and started talking about what he calls "erotica." I call it smut. It's amazing, really. I lost interest in that stuff before they let me into taverns; and now the magazines are full of articles about censorship and relatively sane people like Gould are howling about the virtues of freedom. Naseby claimed Paleologue and Gussie were going to make a dirty movie for him. Possible, I suppose, but Paleologue has always bested Naseby. Then Naseby tried to talk me into doing some erotic etchings for him. "High tone stuff is selling like hotcakes," he said. "You can really make a name for yourself, blah, blah. . . . " Rave on, I said to myself, just don't shit in my chair.

It was a near thing. He scuttled off holding his ass tight. I think his bowels were going. After half an hour I could smell him all the way down at this end of the apartment. I yelled down to ask him if he was all right and he said, yeah, but it was too bad about the wall. That's what happens when you tangle with Naseby.

I was a bit worried he was planning to stay there all afternoon until Odile came home, but I guess he got tired of the smell. Couldn't even trust me to pour him an honest beer, so he left.

I held my breath and went to have a look at the john. I had put the window up before lunch, but of course Naseby had put it down again. A sort of revenge. I put it up again and surveyed the damage. Oh well, I never did like pink walls much. Who would have thought the old bastard had so much shit in him.

It was still all over the wall when Odile came home. I should have known better.

"My God, what the hell have you done to yourself?"

"Huh?"

"The smell! Christ Almighty!"

"Oh, the smell? Yeah, well . . . ."

But I'd already blown it trying to play dumb. I tried to recoup by tearing Naseby apart, saying I'd always known he was rotten to the core, a shitty guy and that sort of thing, but she wasn't having any of it. Hell, I hope she does go, who wants to live with a secret coprophiliac? And her so neat all the time.

Keep the philodendron flying

When I was just out of art school I lived with a girl for a while. She was a second year student herself, little talent and less discipline, but almost as much arrogance as me. A big blonde named Sally who insisted on being called Sigrid. (Does it say something about me that my women won't admit to their own names?)

We got ourselves a verminous flat and went into the decoration game: purple walls, chandeliers from egg cartons, a jungle of philodendrons and a gigantic ginger alley cat. Named Nebuchadnezzar. Lamps from wine bottles and wine bottles from lamps. Inside two months we were ready to murder each other.

It came to a head on the night of a rot-gut wine and hard cheese party ("and we can make more lamps from the jugs") when I caught her in bed with a dumb stud from a record and bead store. That was the end of the party, of two or three illusions I'd had, and life with Sigrid and her jugs. I never did find out whether she broke her arm when I threw her downstairs or when I threw those fucking philodendrons after her. I swore I wouldn't spend a cent repainting, but after a week I caved in and redid the purple to off-white. Took eight coats.

Ti-Paulo in the old days: Mean. Tough. Proud.

Yeah. The old days. Fifteen, sixteen years ago. I can't just heave Odile down the stairs. I can't lock her in the bedroom until she forgets him. Above all I can't, I won't, talk it over like mature fucking adults. Reason is overrated. Besides, what would any of this solve? I think she's through with me anyway. If she stays, she stays, if she goes, she goes. I can't do a damn thing about it. But if I run into Naseby, I'll castrate him.

Sitting on the fence

I wish to hell she'd make up her mind about Naseby, I can't get back to work with all this fuss around me. What with the show I haven't even been able to think about work for over a month and I'm getting edgy. People think you just work, but no matter what you did yesterday you can never be sure of the white paper.

I don't understand when she's seeing him. Dinner hours maybe, but they're usually business. But she is seeing him, because she's going bonkers. Asked her last night if she wanted to go to a movie.

"If you want to."

"What kind of answer is that?"

"A verbal one. Do you want to go to a movie?"

"Yeah, sure. What do you want to see?"

"It's up to you."

We went out drinking instead. I got hammered and she sipped a few martinis, wouldn't talk, gazed around the room. This morning at breakfast it was coddled eggs and all lovey-drooley, flapping her eyelashes like she was trying to fly.

"How's the head, sweet?" says she.

She was out of the house right smart after that one. I wonder if she's as tactless at work. Spent the rest of the morning spring-cleaning. Place was spotless before I started.

Quiddity

No work again this morning. I went in and sat. Fussed. This show really has finished a period. I have nothing to say about the female body. Not for a while, anyway.

Is it possible I love her? Loving a woman is a luxury I have not allowed myself for ten years. The artist always wants the woman to love him more than he loves her. When her love gets to be less than his, he throws her out. It must be that way.

The above is bullshit. My profession does not determine my mind. If I can't even work through the logic of a thing, I'm obviously losing my mind. Or in love.

Me! In love! I may be small but I'm wiry, grunt, gnash, thud. The next thing you know I'll be going to ballets instead of pool halls.

I love her for her entrances and exits. If she is sitting in here and wants an apple from the kitchen she gets up and strides toward the doorway, not long steps, but tall and straight, and with her head up, perhaps even turned around to ask if I want something. The very form of confidence, mmmm-mmh. Then she trips on the door sill.

Her whole life is like that. Not appearance and reality because both the tall and the tripping are real. She has guts for surviving in that ratty business, brave, courageous and bold, and she knows it. She also thinks she's a coward. Also that she's stupid, clumsy, ugly. Yes, ugly. She doesn't count chars, housewives or the girl in the typing pool. She's enough of a snob to cut Gussie and mean it; but she thinks she is nothing. At the same time. She's obviously crazy.

She's out with Naseby tonight. Naseby's name tonight is Babsie, same as the photo editor at the magazine.

A woman is gone

Paleologue called this afternoon and invited us out for a night on the town. I wanted to go, Odile didn't. Said she didn't feel well. No wonder, with that bruise on her throat. And Babsie always seemed such a sweet girl. So I went.

When I got home she was gone.

She was gone and all her stuff. All her clothes, all the pots of goo. And not a word. No letter, no note, ships that pass in the night, it was just one of those things, a simple thanks, a simple good-bye. As if she'd never been here at all.

Thank Christ the furniture is all mine. And the kitchenware; though it wouldn't be any use to her anyway: the bitch can't even fry an egg properly.

Being alone

I've done it before and I can do it again. It's always the same. The main thing is getting down to work again. Now I know she is gone, all questions answered, I can get on with an idea I've had way back there for a while now. Some of these new plastics. Right on the canvas. Flat pattern stuff. Good time to get back to pattern, design, simple colours, lay off the metaphysics. Good basic stuff.

Trouble with plastic is the smog and the soot get at it. Though they get at oil too. It's this trained notion that things have to last. Plastics: fugitive medium. Have to come to terms with impermanence. Metaphysics again. It gets you every time. Maybe I'll play with some varnishes.

Creeps in this fucking petty pace . . . .

Shakespeare really had it, no doubt about it. I think I'll add that to the work regime, read the whole of Shakespeare.

What comes first is the really shocking loneliness. I've been lonely before, will be again, but it hits hard every time. I'm always surprised by it, surprised I can feel it with my senses.

I moved some prefab stretcher boards into her closet. The closet that used to be hers. They'd been cluttering up the studio for a year. I opened the door and the closet was full of her perfume. So I had to hang up a rag of turps and leave the door open. Ten hours later and I'm still afraid to go near it.

When I went to get some stuff for the curry tonight I was halfway to the check-out counter before I realized I didn't need a pound and a half. It's always the same and you always forget. Chili con carne will last three days now. And quiche lorraine is not as good warmed over, no matter what they say.

But the worst of it is the silence. I worked until three cleaning up the studio and genning up on sheet plastics. Then I started in on *Macbeth*. I was uncomfortable by the third act. That's when she should have been home. When I got back from the grocery store the place was so quiet I put on some Mozart. After supper I finished *Macbeth* and put Mozart back in his jacket. Nothing works, none of these sounds replaces a human being, nothing laughs when you joke, nothing argues back when you shoot your mouth off.

So I went out for a few beers. Students in the cheap bars, ad-men in the expensive ones. When I got home it was a shock to my eyes to find everything, every light, every book, every cushion, even the match I dropped in the hall on the way out all exactly as I left them. Maybe I'll get a cat like the old man. That ought to hold it for a while. A house-trained cat.

So

So I loved her, love her. All right, I admit it. So? I even admit I can't replace her.

Today I read *Measure for Measure,* watched a ball game on TV and listened to some more Mozart. While I was making lunch I listened to an interesting radio program about archaeological digs in Tanzania. Then I went out and got drunk. So I loved that woman. So what?

4

Were there flowers in the hair
of the girl
who danced on his grave
in the morning?

Paleologue wrote a sonnet sequence around John Grilse and the poems were counted among the best of his early work. Critics wrote articles about them in scholarly journals, they spoke of their "dimensions, resonances, spaces." Some even said things like, "The quiet man in his search for significance is a poignant and moving symbol of. . . ." But none of them ever heard about Grilse.

"I got a letter from the Income Tax people the other day," Grilse once told the others over beers. "They spelt my name wrong. They keep doing it."

"There's a place for corrected name and address," Gould observed.

"I correct it every year. No use."

The tax people had written to enquire about Grilse's income. They pointed out that if he really earned as little as he said, then he must be getting welfare and this had to be declared. Grilse wrote back explaining that the welfare people had lost his records; but this letter was lost in the mails. During the war, Grilse got a letter from the army telling him to report; but when he got there his name was on none of the lists.

"I figured that, as jobs went, the infantry was better than some I'd had, so I stayed and volunteered. The second day I went with the others to clothing stores to pick up my kit and my name had been crossed out. I went over to the orderly room and they told me I was actually James Grace and I had failed the physical. So I went home."

Gould was always a bit slow; it didn't occur to him until later to ask where home was. It did occur to Paleologue but he waited until Grilse went to the men's and followed him. Grilse gazed down into the urinal a while before answering: "Oh . . . here and there. . . ." Paleologue, who understood the human comedy better than most, was mouthing the words as Grilse said them.

Grilse was a particular friend of the curious and fantastic couple, Dimitri and Francesca.

"The romantic lovers enjoy his company," Gould declared, "because he is as anonymous as they are."

Paleologue snickered.

"Yes, one can imagine the three of them lolling about in that absurd apartment, sipping their martinis and having a conversation that goes something like this . . . ."

He held up his hands and paused with vague eyes as if working out some amusing parody. The others waited patiently; they waited twenty seconds and began to laugh.

The truth is that as Paleologue was having his joke, Grilse was with Dimitri and Francesca and what was going on was much as described. *This could not be true! People must talk, surely?*

Indeed yes:

D: (Raises his eyebrows, looks at Grilse, at martini pitcher, back at Grilse): Hmmm?

G: Mmm.

D: (Pours Grilse another martini.)

F: (After moving a few facial muscles at Dimitri, looks at Grilse): Have a passport?

G: (Shakes his head, no.)

F: (After a while, to Dimitri): Barrington?

D: (After some blinks, nods once, yes.)

D and F: (Smirks, giggles, blinks, kiss-kiss.)

G: (Blinks a while, then chuckles.)

All: (Coos and murmurings.)

Two days later they drive Grilse out to the airport where an overawed customs man hands him a passport. Twenty minutes later, with Francesca at the controls of the lush little jet, they take off for Tahiti. Three weeks later Grilse wanders into the tavern, slips into a chair and waits for a beer. Gould is mouthing off about a party the previous weekend and Grilse nods at the various points. They are all sure he was there. No one finds out about the Tahiti trip until a year later when, in an argument about pre-historic migrations, he says: "In Tahiti I saw. . . ." But there is no notoriety in the revelation: he has just returned from Finland with Dimitri and Francesca and everyone has accepted him as their travelling companion. Anyway, you can never get much out of him about his trips.

"Well Grilse, how was Finland?"

"Same as Sweden, only different."

They were talking about him at a party once, telling Grilse stories, and the model Ti-Paulo was going with objected that the man they were talking about was impossible.

"I mean, if he's such a nothing, why do you all like him?"

Gould got in first: "Because he makes such an interesting change from the rest of us."

Odile never paid any attention to Gould.

"What is he though? You seem to like him, but you haven't said why."

"Because he is a good listener," said Paleologue.

Odile was too literal-minded to be satisfied but she got nothing better from Paleologue who was always willing to settle for sharp glimpses, knowing the full view took time. Of course Grilse was a good listener, but what else was there to him? What was to be the explanation of the time he would turn up on the wharf at five in the morning to pull Paleologue, gibbering and sputtering, the silly bugger, from the harbour?

"Come out of there, you silly bugger. What you need is a keeper and a hot cup of coffee."

They went back to Paleologue's apartment and Grilse took care of him for a week or so. People concluded, perhaps correctly, that Grilse only wanted a place to stay.

"How did you know I was there?"

"Oh, I get around."

Paleologue watched Grilse carefully that week and came to see things about him. It was this week that went into the sonnet sequence, ten poems which pleased him immensely but which did not really catch Grilse, had not tried to catch him though he was the subject. In that week he and Grilse talked more than ever before or after, but talked about nothing. Paleologue then saw that Grilse was appealing not just because he was a good listener, but as a man who knew things he would not talk about. It was not in his silence when you talked to him, but in his slight smile, the movement of the eyes, the knowledge that was behind them.

But what knowledge? Paleologue from his bed listened to Grilse sitting in the living room flipping through magazines for several hours, flipping the pages slowly, regularly, seeming never to find on any page a picture or story or ad more interesting than any other. Grilse fixed all the water faucets and the toilet. He fiddled with the hinges, handles and catches of the cupboard doors. He got the windows working up and down and from a coathanger made a device that would hold open a paperback book.

"Hey that's great, Grilse, thanks."

"That's okay, I only made it to hold them while I'm eating breakfast."

It was true that Grilse read books at breakfast. He read books at all times' of the day and night. Sometimes he read them like magazines, going through a whole book in half an hour. It occurred to Paleologue that a person who fixed things might be a speed reader, but Grilse said no, he just liked leafing through books. "You never know what you might find."

"There is truth in what you say, old soldier."

Grilse chuckled. He always saw the joke, something you can't say for many people.

But when he did find something of interest he slouched back in his chair, bent the book flat and spent the next twenty minutes staring at the page with a quizzical look on his face. "I was reading the other day about . . . " this, that or the other, he would often say. In his way he started a lot of arguments around the table on quiet afternoons, but once started he left them for the others, interrupting only to throw in the odd line, usually unheard.

As soon as Paleologue was well again, Grilse left in the casual way he had arrived and was not seen by anyone for some time. It was learned later that he had gone off with Dimitri and Francesca to take the airs in Bhutan.

As the years passed, less and less was seen of Grilse. People would run into him and ask him how he'd been, what he was doing.

"Not bad . . . this and that . . . here and there . . . ."

But it appeared that he really was doing something. One foul night in April, while sitting in their rented tower on the east coast of Tunisia, Paleologue and his wife Gussie were surprised by a loud thumping at the door.

"The wind?"

But Paleologue went to see who it was: Grilse, by God, standing there in a sou'wester with his little lop-sided grin showing through a fearsome black beard.

"Me? Fearsome?"

"Come in, come in, how the hell did you find us? What have you been doing all this time? Why, the last time I saw you was . . . ."

"Not bad . . . this and that . . . here and there . . . ."

It came out after some time that he really had arrived by accident. He had been a deckhand on a small freighter which had grounded on the sand.

"A ship-wrecked sailor in our house?" cried Gussie who had only met Grilse once and didn't remember him at all.

"Well, if you're travelling around all the time, you must have a passport. How did the government keep track of you long enough to issue one?"

"I bought it in Paris and it went down with the ship," winking.

"What was her cargo?"

"Usual Mediterranean trade. This and that."

From anyone else this would have meant figs; from Grilse

it might have meant raw opium for the French heroin factories.

It was like any other visit from Grilse. He said very little, didn't bother them, frowned at magazines and went into Tunis twice. After a week they got out of bed and discovered a thank-you note on the table.

"He's the most even-tempered person I've ever met," said Gussie. "The most you ever get out of him is a frown or a chuckle. Do you suppose he's very lonely?"

"He's certainly alone. Always has been."

A few days later neither could recall a thing he had said. They concluded perhaps he hadn't been there at all.

"It was quite striking," Paleologue explained to Gould as they strolled through the zoo one winter's day. "Grilse with work." He touched the side of his nose and considered a rhinoceros.

"Yes," said Gould, "Grilse with work would have been striking."

"Of course, the ship went down, so he didn't really have work at the time."

"True, true, he never could hold a job."

"And what a job! The expense of spirit in a waste of shame is lust in action."

"But what about Lord Jim?" Gould tossed this in with an offhand gesture and a sniff.

It might have been a rattling good argument: "As when the sailor cocks a weather eye at the lowering etc, etc . . . " Paleologue would mutter later. But Gould at that age was no man to argue with, his soul being with his wife and daughter, his mind with his work. "The Quest . . . Traveller . . . the resonance of conflicts . . . the Hunted Man . . . blah, blah . . . ." (Was Paleologue so much better? The poet is poet only when he is writing poetry, after all.)

Paleologue turned on his heel and stomped off to sit on a rock in a field of daisies on a hill overlooking a village where he considered the problem of meaning in action. He considered it for about five seconds and dismissed it with: "Quest . . . Traveller . . . Hunted Man . . . Bah!" He then considered the problem of whether or not Grilse had been in the drug trade and concluded he had been. He was right.

Grilse was living in a luxury flat in Paris once, living with a girl named Denise. Out the front windows of the flat he could see the Eiffel Tower and when Denise was out he would sit in the window behind the gauze curtain and watch the elevators going up and down. He got himself a pair of binoculars and watched the people at the top. After a while he realized he was watching to see if someone would jump off. He stopped watching regularly then, sneaking a peek only in passing.

The flat was on the top floor of the apartment building. He had had to buy the flat and it had cost a small fortune, one of several Grilse had managed to salt away over the years. All the flats opened onto a central courtyard with an archway to the street. In the archway was an iron grille gate and a window into the concierge's cubby-hole. The concierge was a war widow with all the curiosity and meanness of every Paris concierge through the centuries. She was there all day, every day, peering out at you. Grilse didn't mind meanness and was a master at dealing with curiosity, so whenever he went past her window he winked at her. Once, after some months, he was sure he caught a smile on her lips.

Denise was a true Parisienne. She was twenty-two and had come from the Nivernais three years ago. She dressed with flair and surrounded herself with mirrors. Every room in the flat had at least one mirror, the bedroom had three, the living room five and the vestibule two. Denise was mean with money, a consummate coquette, foul-tempered and had small, high breasts with the dark nipples of the brunette. She had a job clerking for a firm of charcoal merchants near the Gare de Lyon.

Grilse once asked her if she would marry him.

"Are you proposing, monsieur?"

"No, just curious."

"In that case, no, I would not."

"No, I didn't think so. Why not?"

They were taking an aperitif at an outside table of a café.

Denise took a sip of her drink, took one of Grilse's cigarettes, waited until he lit it, then played words with him. After all, she had given him one direct answer. Grilse played along with her. It passed the time; and he felt he knew the answers.

"Why then did you ask me the question, monsieur?"

"Curiosity."

"Then I will tell you: you are already married in your soul, you always will be. What is her name?"

Grilse shrugged and made a little frown as he watched a pair of girls go by. Denise was becoming a bit of a bore.

"Drink up."

"You Americans are so gross. You have no manners, no sense of humour, no subtlety. You are brutish lovers, pigs. I don't know why I stay with you."

"I am not an American," he murmured.

"And you speak French like a Norman peasant. Of the seventeenth century."

He was going to say better that than like a petite-bourgeoise from the Nivernais. Instead, he grinned and winked and pinched her leg.

"Let's go eat."

She put on a huff for him but came along without any nonsense. She wouldn't marry him because he was not French and because he wasn't respectable. She had the soul of a concierge. He'd see if he could find her a nice, avaricious young notary before he left. With manners. From down around Pau or Perpignan so she could feel superior.

The next day Grilse opened the curtains and brought a chair over. He had a new tripod for the binoculars and he sat there for some hours waiting for someone to jump. No one did. He wondered if perhaps April was not a good month for jumps. It was a good month for leaving though. He sighed. He had a bit of arranging to do with a consortium of Levantine and Corsican businessmen, then he would be off. He hoped he would be off. He would put the lease in Denise's name. She could rent it out to movie stars by the month (there was already one in the building) and go back to living in some horrible little room in the eleventh arrondissement as the savings grew. Yes, he would see a notary about it, he would shop around for the right notary. Of course, it would prove to her that he was a fool. He liked being thought a fool; it made life a lot easier.

In the meantime, April in Paris with Denise. He didn't much like the out-of-doors, but forced himself to take her for strolls in the Jardin des Plantes, the Luxembourg, the Bois de Boulogne. Best of all were dark, wet days, after a rain, walking past the dripping trees with the air washed clean. On dark, wet days he could tell himself the clouds were actually a ceiling, that he was indoors all the time. His arrangements were maturing.

Then one Saturday, about the twentieth, as they were returning from a walk along the Seine, Grilse had a bad shock: coming towards them, on the same side of the street, not thirty feet away, were Paleologue and Gussie. They saw him and recognized him at once and there was nothing for it but to see it through.

"Well shit, I bet you didn't expect to run into Serge Lorenz in Paris, did you?"

You could always count on P. and G. to get that sort of thing. But could he count on Denise? Damn, at any other time you could calculate that her French xenophobia would keep her in ignorance of the Anglo-Saxon theatrical world, but Grilse had seen Gussie's picture a month ago in *Paris Match:* she was making a movie here. Denise would already be going through her massive mental photo file: it was only a matter of time. Grilse decided on the bold stroke: he invited them up to the flat which was only a few steps away. If he didn't, Denise would be suspicious: a Frenchman doesn't invite any but *co-pains* to his home; crazy Americans invite everyone.

As soon as they were in the door, Denise headed for the bedroom and her private mirrors. Grilse turned to P. and G.

"She'll guess who you are before the day is over. That's all right, I'll fix it. But get out of France before Tuesday, go to London or Rome, stay away for at least six months if you can manage it. If anyone asks, you met Serge Lorenz at a party in London last summer, you were there then, weren't you? Don't ask why. Please. You'll see. Now, where shall we dine tonight?"

They had a gay evening, all but Denise who couldn't decide between elation at meeting a movie star and fury at not having been told he knew one. He put her off with promises of revelations; she was to spend a few nights with her friend Chantal; if anyone asked, she could tell all she knew about him.

On Monday afternoon he found his notary; on Monday evening he met the businessmen.

The concierge of Grilse's building was, of course, an informer. She put it this way: "It was at eleven minutes after three, monsieur, I always have the times exact, this watch was my father's and. . . ." "Yes, yes, but was it him?" "My eyes are no longer so good, but. . . ." It took them five minutes to get the old coquette to admit she knew it was Grilse who went out the gate because he winked at her. Other witnesses in the street told how the man paused a moment on the sidewalk to light a cigarette. As he did so, a large black Citroën floated toward him with the two near windows down and a sten gun protruding from each. The man glanced at them with first a look of puzzlement, then of paralytic terror. The stens were emptied of their clips in five short professional bursts each, and the body of the man, after it finished jumping and spinning, was a bloody mess. The driver put his foot down, the car subsided on its cushion suspension and hissed off. When the police found it three hours later it was identified as stolen that morning from a perfectly respectable surgeon. Whoever abandoned it was either a fool, a braggart or a man with a most curious sense of humour: it had been left in a Chief Inspector's private parking space on the Quai des Orfevres beside the building which houses the Paris Police Préfecture. The car was now made out to "J. Maigret."

The Sûreté took over the investigation because it seemed the deceased, carrying forged papers identifying him as Serge Lorenz, was in the drug business. Suspicion fell upon a consortium of Corsicans and Levantines who, informers said, dearly wanted to kill Lorenz and had only been prevented from doing so by certain ingenious arrangements he had made for a meeting the night before. The mistress of the deceased told of other arrangements which indicated he might have been expecting the stens. But all this might have meant he planned a bunk. This theory was supported by the reported swearing of oaths by the Corsicans (now back in the relative safety of Marseille); by the sanctimonious rage of the Levantines; by the possibly humorous abandonment of the Citroën; and by the autopsy report which indicated the deceased had been an alcoholic for fifteen years, while Lorenz seemed to have been a moderate drinker. In view of these facts, the Sûreté left the file open. Over the years it descended to dustier and dustier priority ratings. But it was never closed.

The Corsicans and Levantines didn't keep files; they remembered.

The next time he was visiting Ti-Paulo, Paleologue mentioned Grilse and the stories of his murder in the Paris papers.

"Well," said Ti-Paulo, dismissing everything that did not happen in his own apartment, "he always did live dangerously. No one who keeps his mouth shut as well as that can stay legal for long."

They talked about Grilse's character for a while. After a pause Paleologue said:

"I wonder if it's that woman?"

"The French broad?"

"No," replied Paleologue. "He used to have a thing for a girl named Nora Noon, but . . ." and he explained about Nora's curious life and character. "I met her on the train today. She talked about Africa."

Ti-Paulo finally remembered the drawing class she had taken from him. "She had something about her, but she was too quiet for me."

After Nora's visit the next day, Ti-Paulo shook his head and went to the bookcase. He pulled out the latest copy of an art magazine.

"We missed it."

"The husband?"

"No, her. The reputation, you old fool. I don't know, sometimes I think I'm a better teacher than I am a painter. Take a look at the cover. That wasn't just some dumb Nora, that was Nora, *the* Nora."

The cover had a reproduction of a lyrical yellow painting with a hard corner in it. It was signed with a flourish: "Nora." It had just been purchased by the National Gallery.

"She's probably here for the unveiling. It's not her best, but it's damn good."

"So that's what Grilse saw: the prediction of this."

"I need a beer."

It seemed that Paleologue was on to something: not long after this Grilse turned up at Ti-Paulo's place, asking oblique questions about the "old gang." Ti-Paulo never answered a question unless it was put directly. Grilse had a few beers and looked morose. As he was leaving, Ti-Paulo asked:

"How'd you manage it, Grilse?"

"With mirrors. Paris is full of mirrors."

"So I've heard."

Walking along the hallway, he automatically reached out a hand and squared up the little address book on the phone table. "Funny," he thought, "I could swear I straightened it this morning . . . ."

Nora did not notice the car following her to the shopping centre. When she ran into Grilse in the arcade she said:

"Why John, what a pleasant surprise. Imagine, after all these years. How are you? What are you doing these days?"

"Not bad . . . this and that . . . ."

The bar of the shopping centre was dark and empty except for a few salesmen with their orders for shoes, stationery, appliances, and a table of housewives with the week's groceries waiting in the station wagons.

"You look . . . even better than you used to."

"Thanks," blushing, "I have a lucky figure."

Women in their forties don't look like that, Grilse thought, not even with health salons, cosmetics, couturiers. And Nora had never been a spender. She really did have a lucky figure. Ironic thought. Incongruously she seemed paler, thinner than he remembered, with the skin of a girl. Except for the lines at the corners of her eyes (the eyes themselves) she might have been in her twenties. He was overcome by the frailty of her, the passivity, the helplessness. But so had he always been, or what was his life about?

"It's . . . nice to see you again," he mumbled and glanced off across the room. After all he had been through she could still make him lose his grip.

"And you," he asked, "what have you been doing?"

"Not bad, this and that, here and there."

They had a chuckle over that.

"No, seriously," he said. "I've wondered at times." All the time, damn it. "I know you got married, moved away. I just wondered."

She sipped her drink, smiled at him, shrugged, the sort of thing a woman would do in the circumstances, but not like a woman; with the minimum of movement, no fussing about and no hint of anger being held back, no narrowing of the eyes. There was still some Notty there, not fighting back. But then, Grilse had never tried to take advantage of her, didn't want to now.

"You see right through me, Nora. You always could."

She made no reply, not even a nod, just gazed at him in her way, blankly and rather curiously, as if he were talking a language she didn't understand very well. And, he reflected, I guess I am.

Grilse ordered them another round. He smiled at her wryly, trying to get his courage up, then looked away, fiddled with the stem of the glass.

"I'm forty-six," he began. "I'm a wiser man than could have been expected. I've been around, lived all over, I've done a lot of things most people only read about. I've met a lot of people too, though I don't like people very much, and I've beaten them at their own games, playing their rules. At least a dozen men would dearly like to see me die, but none of them, walking into this bar, would know me from a shoe salesman. And a number of bureaucrats would dearly like to close some files I'm involved in. But I've gotten away with it, I've gotten away with it all. I'm rich, yes. Rich enough not to have to lift a finger again, safely rich with money in banks that think I'm just a quiet nobody, same as the next man."

He glanced at her, had a gulp of drink, began stabbing for

the olive.

"And you have found," she said after a long time, "that the banks are right."

He nodded.

Then something rare from Nora, though perhaps no more rare than his own speech:

"Forgive me, it was the truth. But it's funny, isn't it, how you start things expecting one thing and you get something else from them. You really can't tell, can you. Things just work themselves out. This way for some people, that way for others."

People too, thought Grilse, like you, for instance. He was so proud of her, but frightened too.

"And how is your husband?"

"The same as ever," with big blank eyes. "He's been good to me."

He believed in you when I was too impatient. He had the peace inside him to wait you out.

"He is getting old, of course. Almost sixty." Seeing his quick glance she added gaily, "But he will outlive me. He is a quiet man, he holds on."

"Like me."

Nora shrugged.

"Like you."

"The same only different."

After a while Grilse said: "I followed you here today."

Shrug.

He wanted her to say something, to be impressed, appalled by his life, by her own, by the circumstances that had kept them apart. Twenty years they should have faced together. Paris, Beirut, Singapore: he had been so alone, often afraid, sometimes terrified, but always so alone wanting her with him, just being Nora. That would have been enough.

"I hear you're something of a painter."

"Yes," chuckling, "it's sort of hard to believe. I even sell some things."

"Your work is owned by over a dozen of the best galleries in the western world, you are represented in over seventy prestigious private collections. You've shown at the Venice

Biennale and the São Paulo. In the past six months you've had shows in both New York and Paris. Any painter would give his eye teeth for the things John Canaday said about you. And I have information about your tax returns over ten years. Financially, critically, you are your own woman.''

When the tears came, Nora did not cover her face, did not turn it aside. She sat and looked straight at Grilse and let the tears run down her face. The salesmen talked about their orders, the housewives talked about their kids and their freezers and none of them saw Nora because the room was dark and they were not interested. They would have been interested in Grilse's tears, but he had his back to them and they could not see.

Alone, together, in the bar of a suburban shopping centre, Nora Noon and John Grilse faced one another and cried, having suffered one another to a standstill.

After passing sixty, Paleologue got into the habit of arising early to lay down some lines before the freshness of the day was off him. This practice he followed especially when at the farm. So it was that he arose alone (Gussie being in London rehearsing) about sunrise on an April day of dramatic clouds. He fussed about rather mindlessly with the coffee, making a big pot to do him until breakfast, then took a cup with him into the bay of the big windows on the sunrise corner of the house, a bright and bracing place to lay down lines. He was working on a longish old man's poem, confident and wise and with an air of sad forgiveness. It had to do with light on landscape, nothingness and Scott of the Antarctic.

He got down twenty-some lines, got himself another coffee and started tinkering with the more gnomic bits, trying them as short lines. Two of them weren't bad and he was getting well into the job when he happened to glance out at the field beyond the pond and saw a man walking down from the woods toward the house. He disappeared into the willows at the end of the pond and came out again on the path up through the garden, coming at a deliberate pace, glancing back at the edge of the woods now and then. He was almost to the house when Paleologue recognized Grilse.

"You're looking healthy," he said when they were at last seated in the living room with coffee. Paleologue had always been willing to lie. It was not often he chose the wrong time.

"Time is too short, P. I'm a wreck."

"You are a wreck, you look ready for the grave."

Grilse stared at him suspiciously.

"I've never liked you, P. I've never liked your wife, or Ti-Paulo, or Gould and Rachel, but it's always been you I disliked the most."

"My arrogance. My luck."

"Your fairness. It wasn't all luck, we both know that. Look at you, an old crock, getting up at sunrise to work. Your genius, your talent, what you will. Maybe luck gave it to you, but hard work did something with it. Luck . . . arrogance . . . just words, P. I'm talking about action. The virtue of your acts. You've been too good to be true. Good artist, good husband: when do you find those two together? You have been the best of several people. You have no faults. And the horrible thing is you're still human. It's disgusting."

"Something very serious is happening to you. Have you come to tell me things? Not these things."

Grilse got up and walked around the room. "How cosy it is . . . warm . . . human. You must be very happy with it." He stroked the wood panelling, frowned at a Ti-Paulo, sat in a window seat and gazed across the pond and the field to the edge of the woods. He winced and massaged his knees.

"I shouldn't be out in the morning. Damn climate. I shouldn't be moving around, either," as he went back to the couch.

"There's a blanket beside you."

Grilse first poured another cup of coffee, then accepted a cigarette. "Stopped smoking twenty years ago. Wanted to live longer. You know how enjoyable they are when they're good. I swore I'd live to be very old. Do you know, six months ago I really was healthy? Eyes going, digestion a bit shaky and the joints, of course, but sound, basically quite sound. I have a place in . . . the Bahamas. Swimming, sailing. Off the booze, that's hard down there. I wasn't . . . well, I was healthy, anyway."

"Then."

"You must know."

"I was at her funeral. Her husband will last another twenty years unless his heart breaks. You never had a chance."

"That's what she told me. I would have helped him into his grave years ago but she would have known. It's all nothing now. I saw her a few times. Old Portable never asked much of her. She came down and stayed with me. More than I expected, less than I wanted. Happiest days of my life splashing around in the water and her just sitting there on the beach. Christ, I've never known anyone who could just sit like that. You never thought of her doing anything but just sitting or making love. What a mistake that was."

"Yes."

Grilse had never been able to get anything out of her about her painting, not anything personal. Paleologue was able to tell him of her first attempts in Ti-Paulo's class, of the strange effect her work had on people.

"Left people speechless. Even the most violent of them (and she did some very violent stuff) had about them an odd . . . stillness. Old people do still things, but few young ones. Gussie bought one and hung it in the dressing room of the apartment. After a few weeks she moved it to the hall because she couldn't make any noise near it. It was the strangest thing. I saw her a few years ago in London and asked her about them, thinking perhaps she could talk to another artist. She was dumb: really, that's the only word, dumb. I've also read interviews with her and seen her interviewed on television and it was always the same. No one could get a coherent thing out of her. It seems to me she was an absolute artist. I used to be a bit that way myself when I was young, but I wasn't doing any work, so it doesn't count. I was dumb-stupid, not dumb-silent. As I worked, I learned more how to talk. But Nora . . . it wasn't that she wouldn't talk, she couldn't talk. Of course, she didn't have to."

While Paleologue was getting some lunch together Grilse walked around the house, touching things. He seemed to be searching out the quality of the house. He would grasp a door and swing it back and forth, cocking his ear for squeaks, shake it to see it was solid, peer at the hinges, jiggle the knob, swing it for heft and balance, close it for fit. He taped walls, fingered the drapes, peered at the moulding of window frames, shook the tables to test the legs. When Paleologue brought in the tray of sandwiches he was standing with hands in his pockets reading along the titles on the shelf by the mantlepiece.

"I expect your fireplace draws well."

"Yes, we had it done over just after we got the house. They had bricked it in when they put in their first furnace. Country people aren't romantic about such things . . . . Milk?"

"Please. That coffee put my stomach off a bit. . . . I like your house. It's . . . ."

"Like you said, cosy. The only word. A lot of people have said so. Doesn't matter what time of year, either."

They nibbled at the sandwiches. Paleologue tried again.

"You should have come here years ago, Grilse. Liking . . . not liking. Those words don't mean much when you're past forty."

"Yes, I suppose I should have."

"But you liked Dimitri and Francesca because they never talked."

"Still don't. I was with them last week in Juan les Pins."

He poked the pile, looking for another ham and cheese.

"This is why you don't like me, because I want to talk. You don't believe in talk, don't believe it says anything . . . or that it says too much. Yet that is why you have come here. You want to talk. At last, you want to talk."

Grilse found his ham and cheese. He held it up before him and gazed bleakly at it.

"What is it about this house? I cut you off, didn't I? You were thinking something else. Not cosy, something close to it. What is it about the house?"

Grilse took a bite of the sandwich and gazed at the wall.

"Grilse, you have to talk now. There isn't much time."

Paleologue had opened him up at last; but he turned the old poker face.

"Oh? Why do you say that?"

"Who is waiting for you on the hill over there? Stop pretending, I'm no fool. I took a look with the binoculars while I was in the kitchen. They have a rifle and they've settled down for a wait."

Grilse put the sandwich down very carefully. He rolled his hand over, palm up. He looked at Paleologue.

"The house . . . yes. . . . Do you have some more coffee . . . a cigar, perhaps. I haven't had a cigar for so long. Havana, not Dutch, if possible . . . . Yes. God, yes. 'A woman is only a woman, but a good cigar is a smoke.' Do you know who said that?"

"Shaw? Wilde? Freud . . . yes, Freud."

"No. Freud said, 'Sometimes a cigar is only a cigar.' The other was Rudyard Kipling."

Paleologue guffawed. "Don't we make that mistake a lot?"

Grilse sucked on the cigar, enjoying the feel of being amusing. At last he began:

"There's something you know, something I don't. I know people are different, but. . . . My life has been a disaster. I did the best I could but it has been a disaster. Not just luck. Something about judging people, events, myself. I have been right most of the time. But when it counted, really counted for me, I have been wrong. Not much wrong, but wrong. Little mistakes that went on counting for years and there was no way to . . . retrieve the mistake.

"But you've always been right when it counted. That's what I mean about this house. Things you've gathered over the years, things from the good times, paintings you bought from Ti-Paulo, not from a store, but right there in his studio. It makes a difference. You can look around you and see your life, see what your life has been, what it is, I guess. That song from the war, 'Little things mean a lot,' I have my little things too, but all they mean to me is the mistakes I made. It's not old wine, it's vinegar. Huh. There's a metaphor for you."

"Grilse, you insist on your ghosts. I can't lecture you, we're past that, hell, we always were past that. You know all you ever will. I can say: go back to your place in the Bahamas. Go sailing, swimming, skin-diving, lie about in the sun. One day a woman will come along who wants to share it with you, a woman you'll want to share it with, even if you can't recognize it at first. Expect the unexpected."

"Easy words."

"Yes."

"You're talking like a poet is supposed to talk. You sound better than you used to, but still like a poet, a dreamer. But what about people like me who had to live out there in the real world?

"Damn it, P., she was a real woman, not some girl in flowing robes running through the fields with flowers in her hair, not some damn poetry girl. She was real, flesh, you could reach out and touch her, she could do things that would surprise you."

"Grilse, she died six months ago. She will never again surprise you or anybody."

"Fuck you, you're the same as ever. I'm sorry I bothered you; go back to your damn poems."

He threw his cigar at the fireplace and headed for the door. "Famous people: what do you have to do with life?"

"Grilse, you don't have to go out there."

But he was out the door. Paleologue went to the kitchen and brought the binoculars in to the writing table. He put his elbows down on the sheets of the poem and focused on Grilse who was halfway to the pond, striding down the hill with his hands in his pockets and his head hunched down into his shoulders. Changing the focus he scanned the wood edge but could not see the two men. He laid the binoculars down, watching, with the naked eye, the bigger picture.

A bright April day of wind and dramatic clouds. Paleologue looked out into it from his bay window and wondered if maybe this wasn't his favourite home. Poor Grilse, he'd never had a proper diet of food in his life, but he had seen the home in the house. Yes, a home. . . . Still, it was always nice after taking a taxi from Victoria, to greet Bert in the lobby, follow him up to flat 4B: "Well, 'ere you are sir, and the missus laid in some supplies for you. Royal Albert tea, Miss Gussie has always fancied it . . ." the free air of London, free and not even so very foul anymore, a pint of best bitter, ducks, oh yes, London was fine for a home too . . . .

Grilse was hit by the first shot, standing there with his hands in his pockets, his coat open and blowing. The force of the bullet threw him backwards; he lost his balance and fell. They fired five more rounds into him. The noise reverberated around the little valley so it was hard to tell, really, what was a shot and what an echo. Paleologue scanned the woods with the binoculars but did not see the men. After a few minutes he called the police. While he was waiting for them to arrive he picked Grilse's cigar from the floor. The end was all chewed.

Dimitri and Francesca did not get to Grilse's funeral; they were relaxing at Sans Souci, their place in the middle of the Sahara. The romantic lovers were as young as ever, and as fluff-headed. All for love.

But Paleologue's cable was waiting for them in Algiers when they flew in for the monthly groceries. Within an hour they were in the jet again and on the way home. (F: "My course, sweet?" D: "265° for the first checkpoint Gibraltar, my dearest." F: "ETA, my lovely?" D: "ETA, 1643Z, my darling." F: "You are an adorable navigator, dear heart, my only, kiss-kiss. . . .") They landed unheralded, at four am. Because jet activity was prohibited at that hour, the skeleton staff was not at all pleased to see them. They were granted permission to land but told that a friend's funeral last week was not sufficient reason for special privileges and an automatic fine would be levied against them.

"Until payment, I'm afraid we'll have to impound your aircraft."

"It's a very nice aircraft, isn't it?" said Dimitri as he wrote out the cheque.

"Sure is. British Specialty Corporation, isn't it? I think there was a sultan in here with one a few months back."

"Mmm, that would be Habib. Pleasant enough fellow, but stay away from him when he's drunk. Kidnaps wives . . . children. My little rabbit, would you show this gentleman through the Zoom-Zoom while I hunt up someone to give this cheque to?"

The official was a good union man and although he was

impressed by the Zoom-Zoom, he was also scandalized by the criminal frivolity of the appointments. Francesca worked her magic on him, slipped him a champagne cocktail, the sight of a bit more leg than he was used to, and left him in a state of questionable mental stability. Four hours later (four hours spent guarding the Zoom-Zoom) while D. and F., their duties done, were flying off into the morning sun, the man committed suicide by swanning from the rafters of Number 6 Hangar. In his pocket was found a note indicating that his death was a propaganda act to publicize his adoration of the idle rich, his repentence for past sins, primarily belief in the work ethic, and to help rouse the people of the world to a campaign of death to the bolshie beatifiers of the banal, this last phrase being perhaps the most complex verbal construction ever uttered by Francesca, a hopelessly banal girl in her own beatific way.

But before leaving, D & F had gone straight to the cemetery where "Sweet . . . sweet . . . John . . ." was buried. In their own private way they said their good-bye to the only real friend they had ever had.

Yes, there were flowers in the hair of the girl who danced on his grave in the morning, crocuses from along the road. Paleologue, watching from behind a yew tree nearby, remarked to himself that they were still young despite their (what would it be?) fifty-some years. Francesca wore a full length gown of floating white silk and her long blonde hair floated in the air behind her. Poetry girl, for sure. As she danced, Dimitri poured them each a glass of champagne and another for Grilse which he set on the earth. Beside it he laid a cigar.

Paleologue heard Dimitri say, "John always liked a good cigar."

They drained their bubbly, then poured the rest of the bottle into Grilse's glass so that it poured over the brim and down into the earth, and then they danced away, floated away to the great car discreetly parked behind a clump of bushes. Paleologue strolled over and stood and looked.

"Yes," he murmured, "he always did like a good cigar."

And after a while he turned and went away too.

5

Sarah's Summer Holidays
(For Eileen Shea)

My name is Sarah Mercedes Jane and I am thirteen years old.
My I.Q. is 163 on the Kinns-Noble scale. The Kinns-Noble
runs to 180 hypothetical top. Let the figures speak for themselves. The T.E.C.C. Aptitude Profile gives me highest indicated aptitudes as mathematician (9.7), musician, conductor
(9.6), lawyer (9.3) and doctor, surgeon (9.3). I am pleased to
record that it also rates my highest motivation in the same
general areas (law and music being transposed), thus showing
that I am well-adjusted. Remarkably well-adjusted.

Although I do not by choice participate in so-called
"sports," I have been forced by school regulations to spend
a certain percentage of my time exercising my body. Fortu-
nately I have been able to concentrate on the less egregious
sorts: fencing, judo, parallel bars, ropes, high bar, swimming.
It will be noticed that they have certain things in common:
they require coordination, they are individual sports and they
are not necessarily (and necessarily not so far as I'm concerned) competitive. This is fine with me, for I am disgusted
at the idea of competing with those retarded cows who must
express themselves with brawn because they have no brain.

I hasten to add, nonetheless, that I can see some point to
exercise: *mens sana in corpore sano*. I have recently become

more aware of my body in that I began to menstruate six months ago. I am not yet regular, but all the other signs of puberty are there and at Christmas I allowed Rachel to force upon me four bras. She has been trying to get me into them since I was nine, but I have refused, I think wisely. Other girls at school have been wearing "training bras" for several years and there is nothing more disgusting than their constant nattering and squeezing and poking. If I sound somewhat proud of myself, I admit I am. I have achieved puberty earlier than all but three of my classmates (cows all) and so have gained respect. This makes life much easier in certain ways. I hate to think of the teasing I would have to put up with if I were among the last. Finally, of course, I am glad it has begun. It is somewhat uncomfortable and, I gather from the books, will continue so for a year or two. But the discomfort is not great and I can safely conclude that the major part of it is over. So far as such development goes, I have only two things to cope with in the future: sexual intercourse and menopause. I assume neither is imminent.

The train has been stopped for five minutes in some picayune burg. Rachel assured me the train would be on time, but of course you can't trust her on such questions. I certainly hope it is on time because all my books are in my suitcase and as it is on the rack above me I would have to ask someone to get it down for me. I loathe having to ask for help.

On re-reading the foregoing I find an absurd concentration on bodily functions. Absurd in that I (wisely, I think) pay only minimal attention to them in my life. But, on reconsideration, I suppose it is as well to have the subject cleared up at once. I could have crossed it all out, but for the fact that I have decided this would be cheating. I am not a keeper of journals, and when this one is done, at the end of the two weeks, I doubt I shall ever keep another. And not being a compulsive narcissistic scribbler, I have given some thought to the proper method. One of the first things that became clear to me was that a journal, besides being a record of the day's activities, even the day's thought, would also be a psychological record. In the obvious sense, of course, but also in the proportion. I assume, for example, that I shall be continually surprised, upon re-reading it, to find that I shall have dwelt upon any number of subjects I had not thought I would. This could be controlled if I were to allow myself to scratch things out. Thus the word for that business about puberty shall be: *stet*. And we shall see. Though I must say, if I find myself continually dwelling upon bodily functions, I shall commit suicide. I assume the countryside allows for a number of picturesque and poignant means.

By comparing the name on the last train station with the schedule and my map, I see that the next stop is mine. Oddly enough, we are on time. I'll try to add more this evening.

As promised. They were obviously nervous of me, but only slightly and no more than I was with them. The main thing is Paleologue and Gussie have never had children. I don't know whether this is by necessity or by choice. She has her profession, after all. In any case, they haven't had any and weren't quite sure how to deal with me. Their general approach was to try treating me like an adult but since I'm not one, they couldn't quite pull it off. But mainly they were relaxed and friendly.

They were chatty:

"How was the trip, Sarah? . . . Yes, they're like that. . . . You've been on the Geneva-Zurich express, haven't you? . . . The strawberries are peaking, so . . . ."

They were amusing:

"You'll need sneakers: we do a lot of sneaking here. . . . (on my asking if they had cattle) Heaven forbid! . . . "

This last I was able to turn neatly: "Yes, I suppose the only cow you've had around here is Rachel."

Gussie's answer was admirable, really, without the usual tut-tutting: "No, your mother hasn't much liked the country since the Anderson's bull chased her."

The place itself is quite nice. They have 100 acres, which I gather is quite a lot of land. There is a garden around the house, rather sloppy, but they're not here enough to keep it up. Along the lane (as they call it) coming in from the road they have rows of skinny trees which, they tell me, are Lombardy poplars. I was only able to identify elms and maples.

The house itself is very nice. It is a lot larger than I expected. I know they are rich as anything (Gould and Rachel go on about this constantly), but I was really expecting a summer cottage. As it turns out, the place is a farmhouse. The land, they say, is very poor, and no one can make a living from it. My first impression of the house was not good because it is rather ramshackle in parts. The front porch is all bent and jiggly and the doors don't fit very well. The floors aren't level and the rooms have very odd shapes. Not that there are odd angles, but the windows and doors aren't symmetrically spaced in the walls.

(It's odd, I'm quite tired. I'll finish this off quickly.)

What's nice about the house is that it feels open and spacious. They tell me they have added a couple of windows and the furnishings are quite spartan. So when the windows are open and the sunlight and breeze come through, it feels like outdoors. The furniture in my room is funny.

Second Day

Already I can see why so few people keep journals: it's simply impossible to get it all down. However, I shall try.

They explained to me that I needn't worry about being tired: something to do with country air. The trouble is I don't know whether or not to trust them about anything. They told me, for example, that in the wintertime there are wolves around here. I thought wolves lived further north and said so. They said, well, in winter the wolves get hungry and some come this far south looking for food around the farms. I suppose it's possible. They also told me the oak in front of the house is at least a hundred and forty years old. Now how could they know that? I thought you had to cut down the tree and then count the rings. On the other hand, they told me the names of some wildflowers and they were the strangest names you've ever heard. I absolutely refused to believe them, but when we got back to the house Paleologue got out a book and showed me and they were right. I felt an utter fool, but they didn't rub it in. Paleologue just kept turning the pages and telling me where I might see one or another of the flowers.

93

Then he told me a story about how one got its name, a story about knights and ladies and a monk. It was a very funny story with the knights climbing up vines to get to the lady's room and other knights climbing down from the roof and the monk fixing it all up in the end. Gussie was there too and we all laughed because he told it very well. But then when Gussie and I were picking strawberries for supper I asked her how old the story was and she looked at her watch and said:

"About an hour and a half."

"You mean he made it all up?"

"Oh yes."

"But you were laughing too."

"Well, it was a funny story, wasn't it?"

I said I thought it was mean of Paleologue to make up things and not say they were made up. I mean, it makes a difference whether something is true or not. I asked her how she was able to tell when he was telling the truth and she said,

"Oh I never try."

I suppose what it amounts to is that I can't believe her either.

One thing I did believe her about was getting a pair of jeans. Rachel bought me three pairs of tailored slacks for the visit. I came down to breakfast wearing a pair and Gussie just glanced at me and said, "Well, I guess you'll want to come into the village with me to buy some jeans." I consider jeans rather vulgar, but they are practical and it puts Rachel's nose out of joint. Stupid little town and the jeans don't fit very well, but I'm above such things.

Paleologue and Gussie really are very nice. They're used to me and they really do get away with treating me like an adult. In that, they're unique. They sort of pay attention to me and don't pay attention to me. Both in the right places. And they laugh so much! I can't say how often I was laughing today. They laugh when they're alone together: I could hear them laughing in their bedroom a few minutes ago. I was worried they were laughing at me. Maybe, but I don't think so. I hope not, anyway.

Third Day

I haven't read a thing since I've been here. I suppose I could plead that "country air" nonsense, but the truth is there's so much to do. It began before breakfast when Gussie took me for a swim in their pond. Again: before breakfast. It was odd so early in the morning. The pond even looked different. Gussie explained it was the mist and seeing everything with the light coming from a different direction. She also said she wanted to get me away from the house because Paleologue wasn't finished working. I was wondering when he worked. She says sometimes he goes back to the study after breakfast too, but he likes to work "while the morning freshness is on him."

They sure have strange breakfasts, too. No bacon and eggs. Fresh strawberries and cream. Then a fish called a kipper. It smelled terrible, but I was determined to eat it no matter what. Oddly enough, it was very nice. (I'll get Rachel with this somehow.) Gussie had to show me how to take the bones out. And we had toast and marmalade. The marmalade came in a funny bottle without a label and when I asked what had happened to the label she said there had never been one because Paleologue made it! I made her show me the recipe and sure enough, there were recipes for making jams and jellies at home. Even a thing called "conserve" that you can't buy in stores. But the worst thing was the business about the kippers. She said you didn't catch them, you picked them. She said they only eat seaweed and they come in close to shore to get it. The way you pick them is to find a bay with a sand bar across the mouth and then when the tide goes out the kippers get trapped. The best kippers are the ones picked just before the tide comes back in because when they find they're trapped they eat themselves to death and so become plump and succulent. She said it was the seaweed that gave them their brown colour. She said they get their name because the best ones are caught in a place in Newfoundland called Kippens. Of course I didn't believe any of this, so she went and got an atlas and showed me and there was a place called Kippens. Paleologue hadn't said anything through all this so I asked him if she wasn't making it all up and he said:

"Of course. You mustn't believe a word she says. She's only an actress and actresses don't have real lives, they can only pretend."

"But don't poets pretend?"

"Not the good ones."

"And I suppose you're one of the good ones?"

"The best."

"So you say."

"So all poets say."

So anyway, I asked him where they did catch kippers and he said they didn't catch kippers, because kippers are made from wheat. He said there used to be a fish called kipper that they caught in Scotland and that's why they're called Scotch kippers and he showed me the package they came in and it said Scotch kippers. Anyway, he said the kipper became extinct because of pollution and overfishing, so now they make fake ones from ground oatmeal and ordinary fish and food colouring and Scotch whisky. I figured I had him there and asked him where the bones came from and he laughed and said did I think those were real fish bones? I said yes, and he said had I ever found it so easy to take all the bones out of a fish before? Well, I had to admit I hadn't so I asked Gussie if he was telling the truth and she said yes, you could always believe him, but you could never believe her. I pointed out the logical paradox in that: if she always lied, how could I believe her now? She said she only lied when it didn't matter. I can see why she's an actress, she was so convincing. Anyway, after breakfast I looked up kipper in their fly-by-night (which is what they call their encyclopaedia) and found out the truth. I don't mind them teasing me like that, really I don't, but the thing went on for so long, and it seemed as if they were both against me, almost like being back at school, except that at school I'm more intelligent than any of the others. It's not that they were mean or anything, but I hope they don't do it very often.

I should say, though, that they seem to do it to everyone. Around noon a farmer came to bring them some cucumbers (he called them "cukes") and when Gussie introduced us she said I was Sarah, Duchess of Middlesex. The farmer said she was kidding him because he had met the Duke and Duchess last summer and Gussie frowned at him and winked at me and said ever so solemnly:

"Poor dear, that's true, but they died in a car accident in Nice a month ago and poor Sarah here is now a duchess and alone in the world."

She said I was still in shock and liable to burst into tears unless treated with respect, so he should call me "Your Ladyship" whenever we met. So I pretended I was ready to have a relapse right on the spot and he said,

"I beg your pardon, your Ladyship. Terrible thing about your parents. Sincerest regrets. Always said them Froggies couldn't drive."

I would have given him a curtsey for that except that I was laughing. And it's kind of hard to curtsey in jeans. Besides, I don't curtsey to anyone, not even for a nice person like Nathaniel which is what he said his name is. (I have got to stop using "nice"; there must be something better.) Nathaniel talked in a very strange way, like farmers on television or in movies, except that it sounded real, because it wasn't overdone.

"Yep, she's a hot one, all right." (Talking about the weather.)

"Strawberries *is* about done." (And he pronounced it "*Straw* breeze" and pronounced "about" and "done" in strange ways.)

He had odd phrases, too. Idiom, that's it. One that kept me puzzled was "Shank's Mare." From the context it seemed he was talking about a man named Shank's who owned a rent-a-horse, except that it didn't make sense. There was no point asking anyone but I found it in the dictionary. (While looking for it I found "mare's nest"; very pleasant idiom.) (Hah! Avoided "nice.")

Other things I did:

1:00-2:00: Read about astronomy in the fly-by-night.

2:00-4:00: Paleologue and I went birdwatching. I had Gussie's binoculars. I have looked at bird books and so far as I could tell, the beautiful ones always live somewhere else. But I found out I was wrong (in a way): when you get to see a bird up close with binoculars they are all beautiful. I saw some goldfinches, a downy woodpecker, three cedar waxwings all together in a berry tree, much more beautiful than any of the illustrations, barn swallows, crows, red-wing blackbirds, and a whole lot of sparrows. There are pages of sparrows in the bird book all looking much alike. I also found out that those sparrows around the city are not sparrows at all, but weaver finches.

When we got back from birdwatching Gussie was in the garden sunbathing and she wasn't wearing the top of her bathing suit. She has very pretty breasts, small and with pink nipples. I hope mine will be like hers when they grow, and not like Rachel's. Rachel has breasts like melons and they hang down and her nipples are brown and disgustingly big.

4:00-6:00: We went for a swim in the pond and Gussie left her top off. The pond was made for them. It used to be just a little brook, but when they bought the place they had a dam built and now there's a long pond and a little waterfall over the dam. They have a diving board and a raft. I really enjoy swimming and I was thinking I'd take it up more seriously next fall, but the cows who swim always look like bloated slugs. I saw a slug today under a log, and that's exactly what they look like.

6:00-7:00: We had lobster salad. There was frozen lobster in the freezer and I picked the salad stuff from the garden: lettuce, radishes and little carrots no bigger than a finger. Gussie had home-made mayonnaise. It was yellow instead of white and tasted very good, but odd. I had a glass of wine.

Paleologue was going to show me the stars tonight but there was a thunderstorm about suppertime and it rained after, so we sat on the verandah and talked. It is so odd, really. Paleologue talked about the thunder being the voice of god. I thought at first he was trying to tease me because children and adolescents generally believe in a god, so I was ready to get angry, but I soon realized he was talking to both of us and just making it all up. Then it was all right. I don't mind made-up things just so long as I know where I stand. But . . . .

After a time he got onto a story about Zeus, Juno, Artemis and Athene. This I did object to, pointing out, quite correctly, that Juno was the Roman name for Hera and that, to be consistent, he should keep them all Greek. He said that, oh well, Juno had heard that Diana was going over to Greece for some hunting, so she went along to buy some retsina wine. I then said there were two things wrong with that: (a) when Juno crossed the Adriatic she would have changed her name to Hera and (b) Diana was already in the story under the name of Artemis. He kept trying to cover up for about ten minutes, but he had to admit I was right. What really annoyed me was that somehow I was made to feel as if I had ruined the story. I thought they were above such petty feelings. I mean, if he can't even get the names right, what kind of a poet can he be?

So I came upstairs to do the journal for the day. Now it's done.

Fifth Day

No day four. Not that there wasn't any day four, but that there was too much of it: a visit with Ti-Paulo the painter.

Before we got there we stopped off at an auction. It was just a farmhouse and they were selling all the machinery and all the furniture and junk inside it. Paleologue bought an ugly lamp and Gussie said some of the stuff was nice but the prices were too high because the dealers were out "like flies around a cow's arse" as she put it.

We got to Ti-Paulo's place about four o'clock. It isn't really his, it belongs to Dimitri and Francesca. I've never met them, but I gather they are beautiful and stupid and rich. Vapid, that's the word. The house is certainly rich. It was obviously designed by an architect. It is all angles and square edges, with stained wood and stone and odd windows in odd places. Looking at it from the outside you can't tell where the rooms will be. The wood is all expensive and the furniture is made of wood and held together with pegs. Everything like bookcases and windowseats and the sound system is all built into the walls. There are paintings everywhere and Ti-Paulo says they're worth "a fucking fortune." That's why they let him stay here every summer. The last anyone heard of them they were in the Keeling Cocos Islands in the Indian Ocean.

Ti-Paulo's mistress is quite beautiful which is not surprising since she used to be a fashion model. Her name is Jeannine or Genine or something like that. She is one of the most obvious neurotics I have ever seen. (Gussie and Paleologue were saying on the way that she's the eighth one in a row Ti-Paulo has had that's exactly the same.) You can read her mind just by watching her. She more or less hates Gussie and thinks Gussie hates her, but sometimes she isn't sure, because in fact Gussie doesn't hate her and is in fact quite friendly. So Jeannine can't figure her out and hates her in a wavering sort of way that is obviously part jealousy. She also isn't sure of Ti-Paulo's love (sensible of her), and of course he is hard to get along with, being temperamental and capable of saying very cruel things. But he only means to tell the truth (refreshing thing in people) and a moment later is quite affectionate, so she decides he does love her and begins panting like a dog. But she is also in love with Paleologue because he is good to her and she thinks he would always be good to her. The thing about Paleologue is that he is good to everyone because he likes everyone. That makes him sound like a cream puff, but he seems to like people because of their faults, not despite them. That's stupid—a fault is a fault, isn't it?—but that's the way he thinks. Anyway, although he is pleasant with Jeannine he would be bored with her in no time. Frankly, I can't see why Ti-Paulo puts up with her either. All neurotics are utter bores. Like Gould and Rachel.

She had a lot of trouble with me. She couldn't decide whether to treat me as a child or as an adult. She looked at me and decided I was a child, then saw I was wearing a bra and decided I was an adult, then figured it was padded so I was a child, so she said,

"My, my, and who is the young lady?"

To which I replied,

"I'm Sarah, Gould and Rachel's daughter. You must be Jeannine. How do you do?" (All spoken in an off-hand, confident tone.)

That really flustered her, so I pursued my advantage by remarking that the architect of the house had obviously stolen a number of his ideas from Frank Lloyd Wright and hadn't stolen the right ones. That shut her up for good and for the rest of the day she pointedly ignored me but studied me out of the corner of her eye when she thought I wasn't watching. Neurotics are not only bores, they're hopeless fools.

Ti-Paulo is much more difficult to deal with. When he met me he said,

"Huh, so you're Sarah. You'll have your mother's body all right, but twice her brains. Pleased to meet you, though it'll be a miracle if you aren't a little bitch."

I suppose he has a point. If I were stupid enough to pay any attention to the ravings of those two I probably would be a bitch. They certainly try hard enough to make me one, and frequently call me a bitch. However, I refuse to become an object of wish-fullfillment.

Anyway, I said to him,

"I expect it's possible. But if I have anything to do with it, like-mother-like-daughter will not apply in this case. Anyway, the old bitch isn't here."

So he said, "Right." You can always tell who has spunk and who hasn't. I think my system is a very good one for putting fools in their places. Whoever comes out of it is usually a reasonable excuse for *homo sapiens.*

The most interesting part of the visit was an hour I spent with Paleologue and Ti-Paulo in the studio. Ti-Paulo was showing him the work he'd been doing. Gould and Rachel always make a great thing out of knowing artists, but I don't think they really know anything. They always use abstract terms; Ti-Paulo and Paleologue were much more homey about it. They started talking about whether or not they needed tax accountants because artists can get a lot of deductions, which isn't the way I thought about artists. But in talking about the work it was the same:

"That's a strong thing, eh? That lady could swing a sledge-hammer."

"Yeah, the umber in this patch here pulls its load."

"Comes of painting in the morning. Same with writing. Morning for strength."

And another one, from Paleologue:

"Very neat the way you've hidden that ear. Looks quite

natural, really. Good rhythm."

"Yeah, I get a twinge of guilt about it every now and then. Painted an ear last November and ruined a perfectly good picture. If God had wanted artists to paint ears, he would have put frames around them." (This last was spoken to me.)

Now that is a piece of worthwhile information. Later I went through the pile of art books downstairs and found one of Renaissance portraits: out of 96 portraits, 88 had the ears hidden.

There was another interesting thing too. Gould and Rachel have a couple of paintings by Ti-Paulo, a plastic thing, the portrait of Rachel and a nude. I asked Gould once if Ti-Paulo had used a real woman to model for it and he said he expected so. So then I asked, since Ti-Paulo had a naked woman in his studio, did he have intercourse with her? Gould said he didn't know. But, I said, didn't artists have intercourse with a lot of their models, because as I understood it, the naked form arouses people sexually. Gould got that far-away look in his eyes, the kind that means I have asked a serious intellectual question that all the child-raising books say he is supposed to answer, but also the kind that makes him want to strangle me. He talked about pure beauty and so on and how painters get used to it, but you could see there was more to it than that. In any case, Paleologue and Ti-Paulo were talking about a nude and I found out. She came down from the city for a few days while Jeannine was in town working. I was just going to ask when Ti-Paulo said, "Yeah, very sensual body, very good lines. Too bad she's such a lousy lay."

So that settled that question. It had an interesting sequel. Ti-Paulo went on to say that he didn't use models much because they were too expensive and in the summer when they had to come out to the place there were always personal difficulties. So I suggested he could use me but he said I was too skinny, skinny women had been last year. So, as a joke of course, I said perhaps he could lay me anyway. Dead silence. Really, I am constantly amazed at the reactions you get from adults just by mentioning sex. At last he said, well the law sort of frowned on laying thirteen-year-olds. I said I thought paint-ters didn't pay much attention to the law, and he might get some inspiration from the experience and do something as good as *Romeo and Juliet* or *Lolita.* He said Lolita and Juliet were a different kettle of fish and I said, you're damn right they were, they both carried around their brains in their training bras. Then came the interesting part: he decided it was time to stop fooling around and really blast me. Now no adult has ever successfully blasted me. Gould and Rachel, for example, swing between attempts to "be reasonable" and threats of mayhem on my life and limbs. So I was curious to see how Ti-Paulo would do it. Directly is the best word, I think. Charmingly is the next best. He first established that I was playing games and he didn't want to play. Then he warned me that the game was more dangerous than I thought because there were adults who would call my bluff and there was lots of trouble in it that I couldn't even guess at, because, no matter how smart I was, I was inexperienced and there's no substitute for experience in these matters. I considered saying, well why was he criticizing me for seeking the experience and I considered crying, but decided instead to smile sweetly and keep my mouth shut. I gather from things Gussie and Paleologue were saying on the way over that when Ti-Paulo is giving speeches he has a technique of crushing his opposition: he gets enraged and if the opposition continues to disagree he gets even more enraged and simply shocks them into silence. So I thanked him politely for his advice and said I would consider it carefully. Adults can always be bought off with compliments.

I can't be bothered describing the meal in detail, but it was excellent. Seven courses and a different wine with every one. Ti-Paulo cooked the whole thing himself because apparently Jeannine can't even fry an egg. But the interesting thing about the meal was that it was all the things Gould and Rachel want their meals to be but never are. Full of interesting conversation, for example. The kitchen and dining area are only separated by a counter, so Ti-Paulo was able to stay in on things even when he was doing the next course. Rachel and Gould want to have good conversations during the meals, I've heard them say so. But they haven't much to say to one another, so they are stuck with me. They want me to be cultivated and to have a "communicative relationship" with me. I am doing quite well cultivating myself and of course, the truth is they don't really want to communicate with me at all. What they want is for me to listen to them. Their idea of a "discussion" (which is what they call an argument) is for all of us to give our views on a given subject. I am then either to acknowledge the errors in my stand or to retreat from it with merely nominal objections. In other words I am always wrong unless I agree with them. But the point of any "discussion" is that everyone must be willing to have his mind changed by the others, or at least be willing to agree to disagree. With Gould and Rachel I am supposed to be like one of those jerks in Plato's *Republic* who keep saying, "Yes, Socrates," "I agree, Socrates," "A very good point, Socrates. What a misguided and arrogant little thirteen-year-old bitch I have been, Socrates." The old turd. Of course, neither Gould nor Rachel is Socrates, in fact, not even the two of them put together. And even then, lots of people have disagreed with the things Plato has Socrates say. (I admit I am enraged. Just thinking of those two fools. I also admit I haven't read the *Republic,* it's a bit difficult yet, but I have looked through parts of it because once Rachel said, "Yes, Socrates," to Gould and I asked where it came from.) Anyway, the thing about Gould and Rachel is that although they know I'm intelligent they can't believe that I can know better than them on any subject at all. Every argument comes down to what they believe and why they are right. It's not even any use pointing out that they change their minds, that what they call the truth today was falsehood yesterday. They . . . .

Four dots and to hell with them. I don't want to talk about them anymore.

At Ti-Paulo's we had a real discussion and my views were respected. Everybody's views were respected. Everybody "lost" some part of an argument. Everybody won. We talked about all kinds of things: World War II, politics, mediaeval altar pieces, Tolstoy, fashion, ambition, history. And it was friendly. I don't mean everyone was saying "After you, Alphonse," because there was lots of shouting, especially Ti-Paulo and Gussie, but people said things like, "Yeah, you have a point there. I don't know. But what if. . . ." Be one hellish cold Sunday in August before you'd ever hear Gould and Rachel saying that.

My big scene was in an argument about education. They were talking about free schools and how good they were and how awful the public school systems are. Now the thing about adults and education is they've forgotten what it was like in school. And no amount of imagination can make up for it. So I asked them if they had ever gone to a free school and none of them had. Ti-Paulo had taught in one for a winter. Well I have been and it was a total disaster. All these idiotic social worker types trying to "relate" all the time and all of them hopeless neurotics themselves. Give me the public schools anytime. In public schools all you have to do is learn their stupid rules and keep your mouth shut. Any idiot can pass. If you do that they leave you alone and you can get on with the job of actually learning something. Also, kids in public schools get to be better friends, because there are more potential friends to choose from, and you don't have to spend so much time with them, something that always kills a friendship. Of course, I know they're not perfect, in fact they're lousy, but the thing is, they leave you alone if you play the game, and anyone with any strength of character can live a decent life. But go to a free school and everyone has to be laughing or crying or hugging and generally being enthusiastic about things all the time. I admit I had some bad luck, I was interested in physics that fall. Science is always trouble in a free school. The (ho-ho) science resource person didn't know much more than I did, he hadn't studied or even thought about physics for five years, he was breaking up with his wife (that is, she was leaving the idiot) and every time I tried to talk about physics he would want to talk about relating to the physical world and why I wanted to do it. So I gave up on him and wrote Gould and Rachel a list of books to send me. This is officially approved of: I would be doing my own research. So I got myself a little room and started to go through the books. Sir Arthur Eddington, Sir James Jeans, that sort of thing. All day. With the door closed. Ha! Drove them crazy. Imagine, a kid who actually wasn't dying to join them in their silly games. The first few days a couple of people opened the door, looked in, saw I was busy and said, "Oh, sorry," and went away. But then the "resource people" and the operators started dropping in, by ho-ho accident, and, ho-ho, wouldn't I like to talk about what I was reading? So I told them. Bluntly. No, I fucking well would not and would they get the fuck out. The crux of the problem was that if a student really could do without the others, if she really could plan her own education, then the school was irrelevant. Nothing lays it on the line as clearly as a demonstration of irrelevancy. Especially neurotics. Do it brutally enough and they'll commit suicide. They tried friendly little chats in the hallway, they tried ignoring me, some of the kids tried bothering me with noise. I knew I was getting them: tears and struggle sessions late into the night. So at the Friday evening meeting I was very cheerful, pretended I didn't know a thing. Laughed and whistled with the best of them. After the business was finished (business at free schools consists of endless arguments about who does the dishes) they said the subject for discussion was "individual initiative and group involvement." They weren't going to get out of it that easily. I said, "Fine, let's get it out in the open. You're talking about me." Protests, the liars. "Look, it's simple. I'm quite willing to involve myself with anyone who knows something I want to know. But as far as I can see, you're all ignorant." And so on. By the time I was finished the science resource person was crying and everyone was in a great flap. Beating of breasts, tearing of hair. So I said, "Fine, everyone's going to be friendly with Sarah. Everyone is going to be polite. No one is going to try forcing me into the drama group, or the pottery class or the grubby finger-painting. The fucking jug band is going to play somewhere else and leave me in peace. And until someone here can explain to me something about *Principia Mathematica* I am to be left entirely alone . . . ."

I'm getting enraged again. Those idiots.

Anyway, that's a small part of what I said during the fish course (*truite meunière*). When I finished, there was a long silence. Then Ti-Paulo said, well, there was no denying my points: True, not every free school is Summerhill and Russell himself blew it trying to run a free school and free schools did tend to concentrate on the humanities and social sciences and that emotions get a bit charged in isolated situations. However, this didn't mean that the free school idea was bad. It was always hard to get good teachers and also, I was exceptionally intelligent.

"You see," he said, "the focus of free schools is on emotional development. The public schools operate at very low denominators and have morally, politically and emotionally stultifying curricula. The free school . . . ."

"Look, I know all that."

"Well," and a list of apologies and hold your chair, "you think you're in pretty fine shape, but these things have a way of sneaking up on you from behind. You beat them, and you were right, but they were a vulnerable crew. Beware of your own vulnerabilities."

"Okay," I said, "I see what you mean. But I know there are things I don't know. That's true of anyone my age."

So he replied, "Well, I don't say you're wrong, I just say think about it."

So I said I would and we talked about other things.

That country air again: I slept all the way home.

God. Pages and pages and I haven't even written a word about today. After midnight. Paleologue and Gussie asleep an hour ago. Swam. Watched birds; saw a least fly-catcher and a hawk I couldn't identify (a buteo), a hairy woodpecker (I think), a throng of the usual junk. Good dinner. Talk this evening on the verandah about living in Europe. I want to live in Paris. I will, too.

I told Paleologue and Gussie about writing a diary—they wouldn't try to read it; Rachel would—and they told me Samuel Pepys had a way of ending his that was rather neat. And so to bed. Except I'm already in bed.

Sixth Day

Gussie has gone to town for the day. Back tomorrow. When you see her around the house, you forget that she's important and busy, because she seems so much like an ordinary person. When she left she said to me, "Now don't you try charming

107

him with your young body; he's busy and can't afford the time for an affair." She was joking, of course, but I wondered about it. It's not the sort of thing you'd expect of Paleologue because he has never tried anything with me. Hugs, pinches, innocent kisses, that sort of thing. One of those emotional cripples at the free school used to do that all the time. Besides, Paleologue is happily married, and I am not myself interested in sexuality. It seems on the whole a messy business. I admit I am curious about it on occasion, but I am utterly without any experience at all and it seems obvious to me that I am too young. Any psychology book will tell you about the dangers of sexual precocity. So I said,

"You don't need to worry, Gussie, if he wants a coy mistress, he'll have to try a book or ask that slut, Rachel."

She just said, "Oh, Sarah."

It's the sort of thing you expect from Rachel in one of her more idiotic moods, but it was said in a different way. (Speaking of Rachel, she called this morning. I could have strangled her, she simply will not leave me alone. She talked mostly to Paleologue, though she did blather to me a bit about hoping I would enjoy myself. I said I was having a perfectly wonderful time and hadn't been sober since I arrived and would she please leave me alone. Then I hung up on her. I think she was crying at the time. Fool.)

Anyway, Gussie drove off and Paleologue went back to his study, so I decided to do some sunbathing and reading out in the garden the way Gussie does in the mornings before it gets too hot. It occurred to me also that perhaps a limited experiment in human biology would not be out of place, so I did my sunbathing the way Gussie does, with the top of my bathing suit off. Of course, the point when Gussie does it is that when Paleologue sits in the bay window he can lean forward over his table and see the chaise longue. "The muse must have an air of the flesh about her," she said.

So I was going to be a muse (amusing the poet) and if I was a skinny muse, I think I did a good job of it. The problem was that I couldn't tell whether he was watching or not. This had a most peculiar effect on me. I mean, breasts are quite natural things. I am not particularly interested in mine. They are merely a normal manifestation of primary sexual characteristics. This is true. I am a sane, sensible and intelligent person and I understand what my breasts are, what their importance is. Now I realize that social mores have an effect upon people. I am not free of them myself. I know it is frowned upon for a girl of my age to expose her breasts to a married man of Paleologue's age (unless it is in a nudist camp.) However, it is *merely* frowned upon, except by religious maniacs and such. I expect if Rachel knew she would be in a great tizzy. Theoretically she thinks she is quite daring; but as I have made abundantly clear, she is a sentimental fool. So the tizzy would be her theory fighting with her sentiment. To indicate my objectivity, I must admit I think her theory would win, but the tizzy would be a long one. Now, since I am legally, biologically, factually her daughter, I can be expected to share most of her opinions, more or less. (Look at it how you will, I can't but be affected by her.) So I should have been in a bit of a tizzy too. I was being a bit *méchant* and it seems quite normal that I should experience the usual feelings of a person who is being *méchant*. And, hurray for the intellect, I reacted exactly according to expectation!

I left the top on until I got to the chaise longue and got everything arranged before I took it off. I noticed I had "butterflies in my stomach" so I sat down while undoing it. Then the catch–which is quite simple, really–wouldn't come undone and put me in a terrible sweat because I didn't know if he was watching and I loathe looking awkward. Finally I got the damn thing undone and lay down at once. Of course, I had to get up again to reach my book. I opened it and was damn near blinded by the pages so I had to get my sunglasses from my bag. Then, thinking about the sun, I realized I'd better put suntan lotion on or my breasts would be fried. Then, of course, I had to wipe my hands off before I could touch the book and on and on. Now, this is quite normal in one being *méchant;* I had expected to be nervous. But the interesting thing was the way the nervousness manifested itself: my nipples were nearly popping off my breasts. I had expected a reaction, of course, but nothing so intense and completely uncontrollable. It is quite normal, when engaging in some action which has sexual overtones, for one's nipples to become erect. My own do for the oddest reasons: having a shower, walking down the street, often when I am in an argument. I find it rather unpleasant, really, like an itch, the sort you always get while trying to watch the least fly-catcher when you can't move a muscle. It is most annoying, really, because I have a terrible urge to rub them. I was able to satisfy this impulse at first because I had to put on the suntan lotion. I was further able to soothe them a bit by forgetting about them while reading. (It was *Pride and Prejudice.*) However, it was all more or less self-defeating. I was unable to concentrate on the book: there was always an insect or a bird to distract me and, of course, like a fool I always concluded this distraction by looking at my nipples again to see if they had relaxed and up they would come again. I tried deliberately not looking at them, but I do not yet have the mental control to separate mind and body, and even thinking about the damn things made them come up again. I must point out though, that the object in exposing them was to see how Paleologue would react, so I kept wondering if he was watching or had even noticed me and so on and that pretty well finished poor Jane.

So I said to myself, Sarah, you're a very intelligent girl, probably a genius really, and here's another relatively intelligent girl, Jane Austen, and she obviously spent a lot of time observing the world around her. So let's see if you can do it as well. (Both senses of "as well.")

So I kept the book up in front of me and pretended to be reading it, but actually just watched myself. The first thing I discovered (rediscovered I suppose I should say) was that the body and the mind are not just connected sexually, but very subtly connected. That is, if I were trying to decide if the bird in the bush was a song or a fox sparrow and if I were *really thinking* about the question, then my nipples went down. But the very slightest thought about them or about anything connected with Paleologue or Gussie or any number of other things and bang, up they would come again. It was really quite remarkable. I stressed the "really thinking" because I would be thinking about them and notice that my nipples were coming up and wonder why and then when I examined all of what

I had been thinking I would find I had actually been wondering if Paleologue was watching me watching the bird. Ingenious. I found no exceptions.

In fact, not only were there no exceptions but I also found that all the other things were there too. That is, my stomach was "butterflying" half the time, my joints were tingly half the time, numb the other half. It certainly makes soppy love poetry clearer: the whole business is nothing but a description of physical reactions caused by a mind conscious of being *méchant*. (I know I'm overdoing it, but that is what a lot of love poetry is: panting bosoms, hot flushes, weak knees and so on. Simple biology. Fiction too. Poor little Jane Austen, completely exploded by a 13-year-old genius, ahem, thank you, thank you.)

And of course, the more obvious sexual paraphernalia. Since I was merely conducting a limited experiment and not trying to seduce the man, I kept the bottom of my bathing suit on and didn't, like Gussie, pull the waist of it down to my pubic hair, what there is of it. But there was, to put it scientifically, a definite genital reaction. That is to say, even while fumbling with the top of the bathing suit I was so itchy between my legs that I could hardly keep still. Of course, the whole point of the business was to be nonchalant like Gussie, and it is definitely not nonchalant to be continually jamming a knotted paw into your sweaty vagina or to be raking with your fingernails a throbbing clitoris. (I notice I am becoming quite amusing about it all: it was not amusing at the time.) I couldn't even rub my thighs together. In the end, all I could do was keep my legs crossed and suffer.

I also realized after half an hour that I was waiting for something to happen. Specifically, I was waiting for Paleologue to do something. He and Gussie have been married for years, so when she sunbathes she isn't showing him anything he hasn't seen before. And if he does want to make a remark to her he can do it later in bed. Of course, my breasts were a novelty to him, and the novel is sexually interesting. And I certainly don't expect to give him the opportunity of saying anything to me in bed. (Though come to think of it, I can't see why not. Gussie wouldn't care and it would sure put

111

Rachel's nose out of joint. Which reminds me: if Ti-Paulo sleeps with all his models, what about that portrait of Rachel? Hmmm. Something like: "Gee Mommy, when Ti-Paulo was doing that portrait, did he fuck you?" That will fix her for a few weeks, the cow. Must do it when Gould is there, it'll fix him for a year.) I've got the parentheses in the wrong place; diaries are so hard to keep straight. Anyway, it might just be interesting (stop kidding yourself, Sarah, it would be a stroke of genius) to seduce Paleologue. Yes. Hmmm. Must finish this though. Thoughts of seduction were not in my mind this morning. All that was there was an absurd nervousness and I wanted to know why it was there. I mentioned I had realized I was waiting for something to happen. And of course something did: the obvious. He came out into the garden. Another love poem thing exploded: blushing is an involuntary nervous reaction. I was blushing like a damask rose, or something. And of course my nipples were standing out like those spikes on the breastplates of a German opera singer. There was nothing I could do about the nipples, but I hoped the blushing would pass for sunburn.

(Big incident. New paragraph.)

He came out into the garden with that funny walk he has, strolling with short bouncy steps with his toes turned outward. He was puffing a cigarette the way he does, as if it were the first cigarette he had ever smoked, and humming in a silly disconnected way. Very amusing and casual, just the opposite of the way Gould would be. (How great it would be to have had Paleologue as a father instead of Gould. But then I couldn't seduce him. The more I think of it. . . .) Anyway, Paleologue was in the garden before I noticed him. I almost jumped out of the chaise. But he did it in the nicest way possible, just strolled over and sat down on the other chaise. I was afraid for just a moment that he wasn't aware that my breasts were exposed, but realized he must have known. He confirmed this by looking at them for a moment, leaning his head to one side, smiling winsomely (the very word), taking one of those silly puffs and saying:

(Cough) . . .

> *Shall I compare thee to a summer's day?*
> *Thou art more lovely and more temperate.*
> *Rough winds do shake the darling buds of May,*
> *But Sarah's buds are firm and do not shake.*

Then we both laughed and everything was all right. We talked about Jane Austen and fox and song sparrows and shrubs and so on. Of course, I never did feel completely relaxed, but it was much more comfortable that I expected it would be. At one point a fly landed on my chest and started to walk up my breast and I flicked it away before I even thought about it, acting, in fact, quite naturally. Of course, I realized this immediately, snuck a quick glance at them and was only just fast enough to see the nipples, which had been soft, popping up like gophers. (So much for metaphors.) Anyway, after a while he said he was going to try to get a bit more work done and went away after arranging that I should make lunch and he would make dinner.

So I went for a swim (with the top still off) then went back to the house to make the lunch. (Cooking is absurdly easy. I made a salmon salad and strawberries and cream for dessert. I watched Gussie do it the other day and there's nothing to it. I've never tried hot meals except chili con carne, but I can't see that there's much more to them. You just follow directions and use a bit of common sense.) Of course, I had to decide what to do about my breasts for the rest of the day. If he didn't mind seeing them, (in fact, obviously enjoyed it) then he would obviously not mind seeing them for the rest of the day. So when I got back to my room I sat down to think it over. I suppose I don't need to add that the first ten minutes of thinking were done with my finger. When that was done with, I felt rather dubious about it all, but decided, what the hell, you're alone with him, he's quite sane, you're quite sane, he enjoys it, you enjoy it, you're not going to get a chance like this in the foreseeable future, so let's do it properly. I'm not going to learn much from those dull books that Rachel is inclined to slip into my hands with muttered apologies on rainy Saturdays. Things like *Sex for the Intelligent Girl* by "the eminent child psychologist, Dr. Monica Menopause," nor from *The times they are a changin'*, ambiguously sub-titled "A guide for the curious girl-woman." I'm also not going to learn anything from "selected and tasteful experimentation with members of her peer group," as Doc Monica puts it in her rather condescending "Introduction for Parents." The male members of my peer group (the females too if it comes to that) are not my peers. At least, I haven't met any with even the slightest pretention of peerage. In fact, the only members of the male sex who have impressed me in any way are Ti-Paulo and Paleologue. And since Ti-Paulo is miles away and occupied with that neurotic mistress, that leaves Paleologue. So on that basis I decided to "make hay while the sun shines" as I expect the locals would put it. What I finally decided upon was exactly what I had been wearing before: the bottom of my bathing suit. I took the top downstairs with me so I wouldn't have to beat a hasty retreat in case someone dropped in. On second thought I decided to take a blouse with me too.

On the theory that the acquisition of knowledge, especially self-knowledge, is a good thing, my little experiment was justified by the time I got to the bottom of the stairs: I found that even my little boobs bounce in all directions. It was quite a surprise, really. I am a 30A, natural enough for my age and build, but not what you would call Amazonian. Evidently I have grown since I began wearing bras at Christmas. For when I went "bouncing down the stairs" I learned the meaning of the phrase. It is a most odd feeling, really. They bounce up and down and from side to side at the same time. I expect the best way of describing it is that they feel like two sacs full of rather viscous liquid attached to one's chest. When they move in one direction or another they produce a slight tug at the flesh. It is not unpleasant, but I expect naked dancers must feel very uncomfortable. I can also see how great cows like Rachel could injure themselves if they, say, tried playing tennis without a bra.

I also noticed, while cutting the vegetables, that my breasts assume any number of different shapes when I lean forward or stretch out my arm. I was, of course, not unaware of this, but I had never been able to watch them while doing anything as varied as preparing and serving a meal.

Serving the meal. Serving it and eating it with bare breasts in the company of a much older married man, and pulling it all off as nonchalantly as if I did it all the time. Really, I think I have a definite air of suave sophistication quite remarkably mature for someone of my age. Sarah, my sweet, you have quite a life ahead of you. This last sentence was from Paleologue when I laid the salmon salad in front of him. To my annoyance I found I was beginning to blush, but that was quickly dispelled when he added: "Yes, quite a charming life . . . flirting with aging poets while your charming little boobs are garnished with mayonnaise." As with the morning, it was the humour that made it all work. We sat at opposite ends of the table, with me in Gussie's usual place, and said amusing things about Jane Austen. Poor Jane, if she had been there I expect she would have burst into tears or thrown a swoon. All quite gay and lively. After a while Paleologue began to talk about J.A. more seriously: he thinks she is a really smashing writer. This seemed odd to me, because although I know she has an immense reputation, I said I couldn't see how anyone could call a writer great if all she could write about were the absurd concerns of silly small-town girls in England around 1800. Paleologue explained a number of reasons and I argued them, though with little success. I gather that both his explanations and my arguments are standard views so I won't bother recording them. The one that bothered me the most was that the feelings of a dolt like Elizabeth are valuable to us and it doesn't matter if she is a dolt. What matters is that her feelings are, as P. put it, "closely observed and accurately rendered." I said I couldn't see why and he replied that, in the first place, Elizabeth wasn't such a dolt as I seemed to think, and in the second, intelligence doesn't have much to do with feelings. This, of course, is right back to Ti-Paulo's speeches to me. They both obviously think I am emotionally vulnerable and are determined to warn me about future troubles. Well, I'll think about it. Later.

We did the dishes together, then went down to the basement to work on the wine. Paleologue has all sorts of home-made wine going and it needs to be tended every now and then. He said it isn't really much cheaper than store wine, because if he's away for a while he has to come back here just to take a look at it. Last winter he flew in from New York for a weekend, just to rack a batch from last fall.

It was cold down there so I wore my blouse.

My fingers are sore. I don't want to write anymore. If my plans work out, I'll have lots to write tomorrow. Besides, it'll be suppertime soon: he's been down there for the last hour, humming.

Sixth and Seventh Day

If a diary has any value, the value is in having a record of what the diarist thought on the day of writing. This diary will have to make do with an account written the day after the event, because the diarist spent last evening and night in bed, fucking.

Dear Sarah-ten-or-twenty-years-older, do you remember that day? Could you write an account of it? As you read through this diary, as you got closer and closer to the day you knew was coming (and I didn't), how did you feel? Do you thank me for the hours I'm going to spend writing it all down? More importantly, how many times have you fucked since yesterday? Hundreds and hundreds? (I hope so?) Do you still love it? How long has it been since you stood in front of a mirror and ran your hands all over your body and grinned and said, "I have just been fucked"? And is the word still delicious to you? Do you remember him explaining that people in stuffy sex manuals have intercourse but that people fuck? It is not intercourse or coitus or even making love. It isn't making out or screwing or balling or banging or planking or humping, it's fucking, fucking, fucking, fucking, fucking, fucking, fucking. Oh Sarah thirty-three, have you fucked recently, my lovely daughter? If not, go out and do so at once. Go out and get fucked in your cunt, cunt, cunt, cunt, cunt, cunt, cunt. You do still call it cunt, don't you, that sweet, moist, tingling (rather sore now from overuse), heavenly (watch it Sarah, remember you're an atheist—no, you're not, there is a heaven, it is fucking and there are too gods, prick and cunt, praise the lord and pass the ammunition) (I've lost the syntax here, so excited, but I've got enough adjectives back there so I'll finish the proper sentence with the proper word) cunt.

To the events: After writing up the diary yesterday, I went down to dinner. He gave me a lime and soda. My breasts, boobs, tits, knockers were still bare. Then supper by candlelight beside the window where we could watch the evening mist gathering in the valley down by the swimming pond. Escargots, salad, tournedos and fresh strawberry mousse, with a bottle of champagne and coffee with whipped cream and shredded chocolate on top. Then we went into the living room and had candles in there and lit a fire in the fireplace and then (I would never have believed it) we danced. Me, Sarah Cunt (my new name), dancing! Well, I still won't dance with those pimple-faced nitwits at school, because they don't dance the waltz, the Viennese waltz, arms around one another, whirling around the room with candlelight and firelight and starlight and moonlight and the light of love in my clear blue eyes.

Now I know what it means to be an artist. I have re-read the above about the lights and my description doesn't even begin to tell how wonderful it was. "Wonderful." What kind of word is that? If you read the word "wonderful" you give it meaning by remembering something that made you deliriously happy. But that doesn't tell about the dancing. (Not to mention the rest of it.) Ha! Feelings "closely observed and accurately rendered." I could get the thesaurus and find other words but that wouldn't help. I suppose all I can do is just tell what we did in plain words.

After the dancing he poured us some very small glasses of cognac and we went over to lie in front of the fireplace. I had to be careful not to drink too much in case it should muddle up my brain and distract me from my delicious task. No, I might as well be honest–or what is the use of a diary?–to be quite honest, at the time I was just about ready to take any distraction that came along. I could hardly talk, I was so nervous: will he do it? will I? will it hurt? what if I get pregnant? what if I'm a terrible lover (fucker, I should say)? what if (horrors!) Gussie comes walking in? what if I just fall over in a dead faint? But none of that happened. We just sat there and didn't say anything, just smiled and toasted each other. He

117

finished his and I told him to stay there and I went and poured him another (oh you cool, seductive woman (girl then) Sarah!) and came back and knelt before him and said, "Your virgin serving maiden offers you cognac, my lord." He didn't say anything, just looked at me, then took the cognac and set it aside. Then he put his hands on my shoulders and pulled me ever so slowly toward him and then we kissed. A very long, tender, sexy kiss. Do I need to describe it to you, Sarah 33. Ha! Then he moved his hands down my back and around into my armpits (I have sexy armpits) and then caressed my sides (ugly word, but I don't know of a better one), rubbing his hands around and around smiling at me, then moving his hands all around my breasts but just touching them now and then, as if by accident and I was going crazy. I didn't know what to do with my hands and it was all I could do to keep my eyes on his. Then all at once his hands covered my breasts and stopped and I closed my eyes.

I am not going to write anymore. I have been thinking about it for an hour. I promised myself I would not scratch out anything and I won't, but I wish I could. I have been crying and I don't know why. I can't describe it. Sarah 33, you'll just have to do your own remembering.

I'm alone now. He has gone to meet her at the train. He wanted me to go along, but I refused. I'll be nervous when I first meet her, but I don't mind. I knew what I was doing. I was alone with him and I seduced him. I enjoyed making love. He made it funny and enjoyable. I thought it would be sweaty and it was and now I know sweat is good. Besides, there isn't any other way and you can go for a swim at midnight and you're all fresh and clean again. It hurt a bit but I guess I had pretty well wrecked my hymen before.

And it was wonderful. The word will have to do. I can see why you never forget the first one. I guess I've been a lot luckier than 98% of other girls. I can't make comparisons, but I think he must be a fine lover.

I was thinking before, when I was doing the first few pages for today, that I would feel triumphant when I told the other kids at school or when I told Rachel. But I am not going to tell them. Apart from the legal dangers. It's none of their business. (It took me five minutes to decide on that last sentence.) I don't understand. It was wonderful and I feel sad. I feel triumphant but I don't want anyone to know of my triumph. It's so odd. Maybe it's because it's all over for me. Some girls at school have already lost their virginity (gained womanhood, I should say) and a few more will this summer, but most won't for several years. (Some never will, poor stupid fools.) It's odd, though. I don't feel any different, but I do, too. Most of the time I feel the same as I felt last week, but then I think of it and I know I'm different. "You're a woman, Sarah," he said to me at breakfast. "Yes, I've been fucked till my eyes rolled." "And you'll go on being a woman all the rest of your life." Trite, but true. I guess that's why I'm sad, the essence of one of the four unique events in my life and it's defined in a trite phrase. I wonder if all women feel the same way. I suppose so. Maybe I'm just sad because my period is coming. Eighteen days this time. Fucked till my eyes rolled and I'm not even regular yet.

They're coming. Sweet Sarah 33, I hope you're happy. Good-bye, wherever you are.

6

Family Lives

Before Rachel had to drop out of university to support Gould's studies, she took a course in art history and saw in her textbook the Van Eyck "Arnolfini Marriage."

"Gould honey, don't you think this is a great idea; having a painting done to celebrate a wedding?"

Gould had been sleeping with her since early in the first term and was no longer listening quite so carefully.

"Huh?"

But she kept her temper and explained.

"This painting, Gould, see. It was done as a sort of marriage document. The 'Arnolfini Marriage' by Van Eyck."

He gave her what he imagined to be the correct pronunciation of Van Eyck.

"Well, however you say it. We're still on cathedrals. How was I supposed to know?"

They argued that out for a while until Rachel got herself sufficiently worked up to throw the book at him.

"Well, I guess that makes it a fucking academic question anyway, since I was going to suggest it might be a nice idea if we got Ti-Paulo to do one of us for our wedding, but since I wouldn't marry you for all the fucking tea in China . . . ."

"Hey, Rachel, Jesus, come back, I'm sorry. . . . Rachel!"

But he was talking to the door.

"Yeah, well who'd want to marry an over-sensitive bitch who can't even pronounce Van Ik, anyway?" And threw the text at the door.

Rachel brought up the subject several times before and after the ceremony but Gould put it off, saying they couldn't afford it. As always happens with such ideas, time passed and nothing was done about it. Rachel did not forget, however, and when at last Gould had his doctorate and an assistant professorship, she insisted.

"A bit late, isn't it, for a wedding picture? Five years?"

"Oh, call it a marriage picture then and stop the fucking quibbling."

"But why now? I mean, why not next fall? I mean, I have a hell of a lot of work between end of term and the end of May."

When he was leaving for England to do research for the summer.

"Hell, why next fall? Why not wait till we're eighty? Better still, why not after we're dead, then he won't have to worry about us moving and screwing up the pose. I mean, let's be reasonable, I mean . . . ."

"Aw, Rachel . . . ."

"No, seriously, Gould, we have to get something to go over the fireplace; every time we have a party I'm convinced someone is going to look up and see that damn horse's guts falling out and they're going to barf all over the canapés."

The picture was a four-by-two reproduction of Picasso's "Guernica."

After several hours they reached a compromise: Rachel would have Ti-Paulo do a portrait of her over the summer and a matching one of Gould in the fall.

"Fine, and then if I decide to leave you, I can take my part of the marriage without having to saw it down the fucking middle."

"Aw, Rachel, Jesus, lay off, really, I'm just too fucking busy."

"And maybe I'll get him to screw me while I'm at it, I hear he's really something in the sack, these little guys, you know . . . ."

"Jesus fucking Christ, Rachel, sometimes . . . ."

"I mean, it's not as if I'm being screwed to distraction at

home, so I don't see . . . ."

"God damnit, Rachel, if I get my hands . . . ."

All of which places Rachel one sunny morning in late June on the platform of the railway station two miles from Dimitri and Francesca's country place where Ti-Paulo was staying that summer, the first of many he was to spend there.

"Hey, Rachel-Big-Boobs!"

Grinning from the open window of the Land Rover, reaching for levers, then the door swings open and he comes toward her with the light, energetic step of the compact man.

"Hey Ti-Paulo, mmmm, great to see you again!" Big laugh, big hug, Rachel-Big-Boobs being friendly and free. Big kiss, too, and a quick cover-up: complaints about the woman two seats forward on the other side of the train, once a cute teeny chubby, now a fat, fading twenty-five, her greasy hair held in a ponytail by an elastic band, the pig trying to control her two brats, Rachel never having had any of her own but, to be honest about it, would have similarly disembowelled the poor woman anyway out of pure Rachellishness, nattering on, keeping her eyes from Ti-Paulo's until she regained control of herself with a cigarette in her hand and lounging in the passenger seat as Ti-Paulo gunned it out of the station parking lot and down the street of the little town.

"My God, I suppose this is the nearest civilization, is it? Jesus, can you imagine living here, look at that, The Paree Bon-Ton, frocks and lingerie, and the hairdresser next door, can you imagine?"

"Yeah, I can. I have to order materials here. The hardware store is well-stocked."

"Oh hell," with a chuckle, "what a bitch I am."

As they left town she cocked her cigarette hand and crossed her legs, the right over the left, a very long, large leg whose appeal was proved at once by the stirring of Ti-Paulo's querulous organ.

"And how are you, you old grouch?" In her best bedroom purr. He chose to treat it as an old friend's purr with a free extra thrown in.

"Not bad."

"Mmmm," smiles and chuckles. "You really look great. Your hair is all bleached from the sun." She reached over to run her fingers through it.

"Swimming. Gets the muscle tone up, too."

"Lots of healthy garden vegetables."

"Green and leafy. Strawberries too."

God, it's good to see him again, he's so himself, so alive, always taken such good care of himself, how long since Gould gave a damn about muscle tone, hell, how long since I have . . . .

She's embarrassed about being overweight, those thighs will be pretty hefty up top there, see if I can get her into the water, knock some of it off her. . . . But she's happy she's here, wonder how long that will last? She's willing to get laid, first time since she got married, I bet, but she'll be coy about it, always gets coy, Rachel does, a textbook case. Well, we'll see.

She came down the stairs wearing a robe to mid-thigh to hide those bulges and a tiny black bikini under it. Smiling, but avoiding his eyes until she got to the bottom.

"I think you're trying to tell me something, Boobs."

"That I'm ready to go swimming?"

"That'll do."

"Lead me to it."

Indeed yes.

Her thighs were spreading at the top, but less than he had expected; and her waist was much better than anyone had the right to expect of her. A good, big woman.

"You're an all right swimmer, Boobs."

She beamed.

"Thrashing along there."

An obscene gesture.

"A bit of practice and you'll be fine."

And a water fight.

Afterwards they sat on the cantilevered patio in the humming heat. Bouncy chatter at first—"My God, the water, the sun, the air, I'd completely forgotten what it was like to feel so completely alive!''—changed after some minutes to confessional—''I meant that, Ti-Paulo, really. It feels so wonderful to be here, the swimming, the sun, it feels like my body is . . . breathing again. You know what I mean?''

''Yes.''

She was not looking at him now, nor at her body, but was gazing vaguely toward the horizon while her fingernail moved over her belly in lazy whorls, the real thing coming soon now: ''We do such . . . stupid things to ourselves . . . and we're so . . . lucky in this country, we . . . have the chance to be . . . healthy . . . energetic . . . happy . . . and we . . . let it slip away from us . . . most of us. . . . '' She turned to him. ''It's criminal, isn't it? But you don't waste yourself, do you? You work at it.''

''Yes.''

''Show me.''

While drinking coffee afterwards, Rachel made a discovery: ''You know, I'm not a whore. Whoredom is in the mind. I'm not even an adulteress. I don't feel any different about my marriage. I have not betrayed him. This thing here is only flesh like my hand . . . or my ear. He can't shove it into me now anyway, because he's five thousand miles away, so what does it matter if . . . .''

Ti-Paulo broke into the long pause:

''Besides, he's probably got his in some other girl's thing. Let's see, it's . . . .''

''The bitch, I'll scratch her eyes out, Gould is such a child, he loves being called 'doctor,' I can just see him falling for some red-brick tart . . . .''

'' . . . seven-twenty-three here, we're five hours behind, twelve-twenty-three, pubs close at eleven-ten . . . .''

''The hell with them,'' trying to cover his mouth, ''the hell with them, I say!''

Just before she succeeded: ''Yeah, the hell with them. Besides, she probably doesn't have boobs like yours.''

''Look, Rachel,'' in a business voice over breakfast, ''I'd like to do a full length reclining nude, something very sensual.

Really do your body."

"My God, you're out of your mind!"

"Yeah."

"I mean, everyone . . . ."

"Everyone will know anyway. Or think they know. The question is whether you want to flaunt it or not. I don't care, people expect artists to screw their models, but you have to live with it."

"Well . . . ."

Rachel had a strong streak of practicality, but she knew her body would never be better. And her first affair. And if Ti-Paulo became famous . . . .

Ti-Paulo had his own practicality, the artist's, which is second only to the mystic's: he decided to do two pictures, the nude with a generalized face, and the portrait, clothed. "I'll do a bang-up job of the nude, see if I can get it in a public gallery . . . ."

Dreamily: "Thousands of people looking at . . . ."

Dreamily a few days later: "What if I'm pregnant?"

"Well, if you are it won't start to show for a while, so it's fine with me. The swelling gives the breasts an unnatural firmness. Unless it's meant to be a picture of a pregnant woman. Which this isn't. And stop squeezing them in that enquiring way, you'll make them swollen anyway."

"You never let up, do you?"

"Anyway, you wouldn't be able to feel it yet."

He was right, of course, but she was sure she was pregnant. She and Gould had been trying for several years and it hadn't taken. They had never gone to a doctor to find out who was at fault, but she knew it could not be her. "I mean," to herself, "I'm damn sure God didn't give me these hips just to hold up my skirt."

Ti-Paulo took her over the way he took over all his women. She was made to learn about wines (Gould had already done this but it appeared he had been mostly wrong), the correct way to chop vegetables, how to stalk and recognize birds, how to cast a fly line, how to identify wild flowers and constellations in the sky.

125

"The problems of photographing birds are these: birds are small, shy and quick-moving. This means you either get close to them by building a blind about a hundred feet in the air next to a nest, one blind to one nest, and sitting in it for three days or by using a telephoto lens which gives you a number of light problems in addition to the usual light problems. The ideal solution is to get above them with the light source behind you and dark shadows behind them. That's why we're going up to the south rim of that gully with a tripod and a very expensive telephoto zoom lens."

"But why do I want to photograph birds?"

"Because you want to accumulate knowledge and experience."

"The only birds I'm interested in . . . ."

"And if you go home with a lot of great photographs of birds, people won't have to ask what you did in your spare time."

"Funny, you know I was just thinking how nice it would be to have a picture of a cardinal."

"Right. Now, to get a well-resolved photograph you want, ideally, a small aperature, low ASA, slow shutter speed and . . . ."

"Having an affair is supposed to make you feel free," she said a few evenings later while sitting by the fire. "Well, it fucking well doesn't. Christ knows, Gould is a bit of a fool, but he can leave me alone now and then, he lets me do a bit of thinking on my own. He always thinks he's right, but he can let me disagree with him. But that's not good enough for you. Everyone has to agree with you, everyone has to live life to suit your convenience, keep the place neat, swim before breakfast—no, don't pretend, you let me sleep in, but you really think I should be out there ticking off my thirty lengths with you, toning up my goddamn deltoids and chopping a fucking onion into fucking fine dice just exactly the way you do, memorize goddamn stars that I'll never remember anyway because I'm not interested in them. I mean . . . I'm me and I . . . it's like arms reaching out from your brain, you know, and they . . . hold onto things or reach for things and everyone holds onto different things and I'm interested in some of the things you're

126

interested in but you're not interested in what I'm thinking about or want to think about. I mean, what do you know about me that you didn't know before I came—and *that* doesn't count as you very well know—no, I mean, what do you know about . . . oh, what I think of the countryside, for instance? Or . . . well, more to the point: even though you've been screwing the ass off me and painting a picture of me, do you really have any idea of what I think about my body? You know, calling me Boobs and saying I'm a big woman, but what do I think about being so big? Do you care? I don't think you give a sweet damn. . . . I. . . . Oh Jesus, Jesus, Jesus God, sometimes it seems so. . . . I try, I really do. Years of trying to be . . . oh, not a ballerina or an actress or something, but just . . . me, all of me, Rachel. Oh Jesus, it's hard, so damn hard trying to figure out what I think about my body, never mind what anyone else does. Not that I don't know already. You never knew me in grade school, thank God. Was that hell, I was such a great ox of a thing, bigger than all but one of the boys even, all knobby knees and teeth and feet. A couple of years they had to get big desks from higher grades so I could slouch down at the back of the room like some fucking great elephant because if I sat at the front all the cute little blonde girls wouldn't be able to see the board, not that they had to, they memorized everything; so naturally I couldn't see the board myself and almost failed grade three, can you imagine, that was back in the days when you could fail in grade school, all because I had to sit at the back and no one had figured out that I needed glasses. Oh that was lovely, too, it was bad enough being an ox without glasses, but you can imagine the ugly ones my parents got me when they did find out. Oh Jesus. You know me, I'm no genius, but I'm not stupid, really. But do you know, for years and years, until I got to about the middle of high school, I thought I was a dummy. A bone-headed, myopic ox. God, I'd rather burn in hell for a million years than have to go through grade school again. You think perhaps I'm proud of my boobs and legs, and you're right, oh God, how right you are. Was I a new girl when I found I had them. No, that's not true, it wasn't just having them. Look, you think maybe you know about fashion because you were screwing that model. Well let me tell you, you have no idea what fashion means to millions of girls. See, even after I got my figure I was still a freak because in grade ten the styles were all wrong for big women and the new ones came in the next year, dresses, skirt length, hair, waist, belts, accessories, make-up, the whole thing changed, not just a small change, but a big one, the kind that comes once a decade, you know, one where you can't get by with alterations on last year's stuff, but where you have to get everything new. And the changes were all in my favour and against the cute little curly-haired ones. Like hair, for example. You think maybe it doesn't matter if fashion says everybody has to have curly hair, the girl just does it a different way. But you wouldn't believe the hell I went through for years trying to put waves in my hair, years when I had to lie on my face to go to sleep, when not just rain but mere dampness in the air was a total disaster and in the john before classes the kinky-haired ones would stand in front of the mirrors smirking and patting their curls and perhaps condescend to pretend to feel sorry for me because the curl fell out if someone so much as turned on a tap ten feet away. But then, oh sweet loving Jesus, it happened, the style changed, straight hair was in and all those miserable little bitches were going out of their fucking minds trying to get the kinks out of their hair. Hot combs, twenty bucks a month at the hairdresser for straightening, and curses, oh my, yes, the little sweeties who had been such cute widdle fwings for all those years could suddenly swear like truck drivers and it was, 'Fuck, Rachel, you're so goddamn lucky, your hair is so long and straight and silky, cummere Joyce and feel Rachel's hair, shit some people have all the luck, Christ, I wish I'd never been born.' Bitch. And I never felt sorry for any of them, not a second. You must have noticed how all those cute little girls who were the knockouts of grade five just sort of disappeared in high school? It's as if there was set time worked out with your genes and that time is the only one when you're going to be beautiful, because those poor little snits were cute in grade four because they looked like Shirley Temple and when it came time to have boobs they didn't get any and they just faded away and you never saw them again. Maybe they'll be cute at sixty, but I doubt it, because they'll probably spend all their lives being bitter about their fall from glory and being jealous of people like me, the cows of grade school, after we started to have our innings and being chased by everything in pants. Oh Jesus, it was wonderful. . . . Let me tell you about skirt lengths and lines. I mean, the hair styles just got me out of hell, my hair isn't all that great. But the skirts, they really did it, they put me in heaven. It's the proportions, I think. You know what I mean, you're a painter. See, when I started high school, no one cared about my legs, partly because they couldn't see enough of them, but also because of all the other lines. My lines were all wrong because all the styles for skirts and blouses and sweaters had these picky little detail work and broken lines, everything perfect for little girls about five-two, 32-18-30. You remember that fad for sweater girls, eh? You think the big bosoms looked best, but if you think back carefully it was only the mother-fixated imbeciles who really like big boobs, because sweaters make people like me look like cows, and the ones who look great are the 32B's with those casual folds and their pointy little tits twinkling out, hinting, not blaring out. But when the change came all the lines changed, they threw out all the fussy details; the long lines, the simple ones were in and the skirts went up to here. And all of a sudden it wasn't ankles anymore, it was the long curve of calf through the knee and into the thigh. My ankles are no hot shit, but I've got fabulous lines above them and I know it. And the right styles for those legs are flare skirts and flare skirts are a glory for hips like mine and to go with the skirt and the hips you have to have a long, smooth midriff or a very simple belt, and those lines mean you have very simple bustlines, not emphasizing the bust because the important things are all down lower. And all of it perfect for me, me, me, all the vertical lines and simple cuts and simple colours and big, bold accessories, no more of those fucking little strings of pearls, good-bye to those delicate little gold chains with their itsy-bitsy little lockets shaped like hearts, Christ, it was great dangly hoop earrings and big brass belt buckles, and I'd been working as a waitress at a summer resort so I learned a few things about make-up from the other kids, mascara and eye-shadow especially, and I could wear it without feeling I was a whore. Anyway, you put all that together, baby, and you have lumbering old Rachel turning up the first day of grade eleven with a summer's pay worth of new clothes on my back, and highlights around my big (wink) brown (wink) eyes (wink) and these magnificent legs (swish-swish) and those lovely big tits (jiggle-jiggle), boy I came striding into that school and in ten minutes I wiped out ten years of hell for me, and vanquished hundreds of little cuties; boy, no one has heard of them since. They're all married to drab little creeps they wouldn't even have shit on the year before. And that was a basketball school and all those great hunks of men were beginning to get bored with those little cuties, you know, dancing with the chick's nose in his naval and all of a sudden there were these great big bombs lolloping around in high heels and I'm five-nine in my stocking feet and all I have to do is stand beside a basketball player and he looks like a human being instead of a freak, better in fact, because he and the chick are larger than life and Rachel was that chick, me and four or five others. You know how they say girls can't be friends? Well that may be true for most broads, but it was a load of shit as far as we were concerned, because we'd all been through the same crap for years and now it was our turn and there were, like I say, half a dozen of us and hundreds of guys to go around, hell, we didn't have to fight for them, we had to fight them off, sweet Jesus, that was heaven. . . . All those men . . . the parties . . . dancing . . . laughing . . . the good times . . . . When I think back. . . . You know, I can just see myself, you know, not from the inside, but as if I were watching myself from across the room, I . . . can see it so clearly, wearing that great gold and brown dress, gold above, brown below, joined on a big diagonal right from here down across to here, cut on the bias, God that dress did things for me, and I'm standing with my weight on one leg, the other one out like this, tall and straight, God I was a beauty (still am, God damn it), and my cigarette up like this and my other hand across and under the elbow and I'm laughing, not a loud laugh, but an honest, happy laugh, God I was so happy to be beautiful, so big and beautiful and happy. . . and . . . Oh Jesus . . . I . . .

130

well, I guess that's one advantage of the country, you don't have to worry about . . . smearing your make-up when . . . when you . . . cry . . . Oh Jesus, Ti-Paulo, why does it all . . . Oh, God, I don't know anymore, I just . . . ."

Ti-Paulo heard the whole alphabet of her life. Everything from Art of Marriage courses ("How to sweat your ass off making your home and your body lovely for Him, Him, Him.") to Zucchini Provençal ("Creative cooking is the shits.") with longish stops at B (Blessed Event), G (Gould), M (Meaning and Me). He only half listened, balancing his A (Annoyance) with B (Bedding) until after a C (Couple of Weeks) with only the D (Drawing) done he decided to toss her out on her E (Elegant Ass).

"I've got enough here to finish off. I like you Boobs, and I'm glad you came, but I've got a living to make and my dealer isn't going to pay me a thin dime for getting into your panties three times a day."

"While we were in town yesterday I went to the drug store and had them do a little test for me. I'm pregnant."

"Let me be the first to congratulate you, Boobs. It couldn't have happened to a nicer girl. And please pass on my congratulations to Gould. I didn't know he had it in him."

"I'm going to have an abortion."

"Oh for Christ's sake."

"I am, I really am."

"Don't be ridiculous."

"Why won't anyone ever believe me?"

Because you don't mean it, he said to himself. But as a precaution he called a painter friend in town and dictated a note to be sent to Gould's London address:

> Gee it seems such a shame after you trying all these years for a Blessed Event and now you have got your wife in the Family Way she wants to have an operation which is a crime of murder against unborn children who can't protect themselves and your estate.
>
> A Well Wisher.

Oddly enough, Gould got a second letter the same day:

> *Dear Doctor,*
> *As your wife is Expecting I think you would want to be at her side because there is word going round the bitch is going to have an operation which is dangerous for said Expectation not to mention her and you having put in so much of yourself into the business (If You Catch The Meaning) will be interested. Also being a Medical Person.*
>
> *A True Friend.*

"Ooo," said Doris, the bit of stuff Gould was shacked up with, "the nosey-parkers!"

"Balls. She wrote the second one herself."

"How d'you know that?"

"Because my wife has about as much subtlety as a fucking billboard. I suppose I have to call her. Damn it all, just when I was getting into things over here."

At which Doris giggled and he smirked and they had a tumble before he tried calling.

"Okay, Rachel, I got your letter, now what's this . . . ."

"What letter? I never sent a letter."

"Come off it Rachel, just tell me if you're up the stump or not."

"I don't know what you're talking about."

"Rachel, I got two letters about it today and . . . ."

"Whaddye mean, two letters?"

"Listen, is it mine or is it that goddamn painter's?"

"Gould, there's nothing, I mean, nothing is wrong, I mean, well, what are you . . . ."

"Okay, Rachel, if that's the way you want it. This call is costing a fortune, so . . . ."

"Oh Gould, don't hang up, lover, I'm so miserable without you."

"I bet you are, now you're home. Is he as great in bed as they say?"

"Stop it, don't, why are you doing this to me? I'm so scared Gould, and I throw up every morning and . . . ."

That'll get him, the fastidious shit, and anyway, it's true, oh
God, I do want him to come home, I want him here with
me . . . .

Two hours later, while Gould was trying to strong-arm a
very polite BOAC ticket girl, Rachel was striding about the
apartment in jeans, heaving chairs about, vacuuming and preparing her speech:

"What the hell are you doing home, for Christ's sake, you
think I'm one of those dainty little blondes you're always
ogling around the campus? Like hell mister, look at these hips,
I could carry ten of your brats and still lug out the garbage
cans, not that you'd notice. And what's the Head of the English Department going to say when he finds out you've fucked
up your research for the summer, you think they're going to
make you an associate prof without results, eh? How're you
going to feed us? Just like you, think you're so goddamn cool
and the first hint of anything and it's transatlantic phone calls
and flying home, God, men, and don't think I can't smell the
perfume on your jacket, Mary Quant, isn't it? . . . No, with
my luck it would be Prince Matchabelli. . . . Goddamn, I will
not be intimidated, he's having a bit and so did I, he wanted
a kid and now I'm going to have one, so there's not going to
be any shit about . . . ."

"Itty-pitty-witty-wooty-wooty-woo, ess it is, ess . . .ess it
is. . . . Hey Hon, look, she's aware of her hands and feet,
see . . . ."

"I'm waiting for the day she becomes aware of her bum."

"She's really developing, even in the last two weeks, eh? I
wonder what . . . . Interest, I suppose that's it. She has this
innate interest in herself and in the world and the interest
focuses automatically on what she should exercise so she de-
velops properly. I wonder what controls the . . . focus of the
interest . . . ."

"The same thing that controls her ass."

"Uhh . . . speaking of . . . ."

"Christ, Sarah, not again, Jesus, baby, you went an hour
ago."

"Oh my God, it's eight already. Here Hon, I'm really sorry,

but I have to get back to the library and get in a few hours before . . . ."

"Oh Gould never mind the fucking excuses."

"Huh?"

"Go on, just give her to me and get the hell out of here before I ram a diaper-load of shit down your throat."

"What the hell are you . . . ."

"Go on, get out of here, I've got work to do."

"Listen Rachel, don't try that fucking martyred mother routine on me, I've got work to do too, you know. Someone has to pay for that new washing machine and I'm damn sure her father isn't going . . . ."

"You wanted a baby, you've got one. Don't blame me if you're incapable of . . . ."

"You bitch!"

"Come Sarah, sweetie, we'll go get a fresh diaper, Daddy's having an attack of the galloping rationalizations, it comes from overwork, you know, ess it does, ess it does . . . ."

"All right, Rachel, all right!"

Slam.

Paleologue once wrote a poem about the predictability of individuals, but decided it was too cute and destroyed it. "Paradox," he explained to Gussie, "is too easy, because it is rampant in the world." To which Gussie replied, "Uhuh," and went on shaving her leg. She was listening, but she knew her man: he would deliver an amusing two-hour lecture proving that paradox was so common as to be beneath notice, he would refute in passing the "What oft was thought but ne'er so well expressed" objection, would show with detailed proof that his favourite poets of the past had seen this and had written accordingly, that his own best work was anti-paradoxical, that this was the true thread of unity through his work, that his most recent work had been moving more clearly in this direction and that planned work in the near future would be the apotheosis of anti-paradoxicality. True to his word, he embarked the next day upon what was to become a four-hundred-and-twenty-three-line poem of utterly unparadoxical directness, clarity and limpidity. True to his nature, though, he followed this with his notorious *Attila in Love* which he subtitled: "A celebration of what both is and is not." When he first met Sarah as a rational being (she was eight at the time) she had just finished reading *Attila in Love* and said she, "found it obvious. That sort of thing is everywhere." She tossed her head at her parents. "I mean you only have to look around, don't you, to find you're surrounded by swamps of arbitrary illogicality."

"That will be quite enough, Missy."

"Really, Rachel, I only state the obvious."

"Get out of here."

"And my name is Sarah."

"Then go play in the traffic. Sarah."

Sarah sashayed to the door declaiming:

> *In vain, in vain,—the all-composing Hour*
> *Resistless falls: the Muse obeys the Pow'r.*
> *She comes! she comes! the sable Throne behold*
> *Of* Night *Primaeval, and of* Chaos *old!*
> *Before her,* Fancy's *gilded clouds decay,*
> *And all its varying Rain-bows die away.*
> Wit *shoots in vain its momentary fires,*
> *The meteor drops, and in a flash . . . retires!*

Slam.

"Bright kid," said Paleologue.

"Yeah, the little bitch. I wondered what she was doing in the study this morning. It was all a set-up."

"I found her quite charming," said Gussie.

To which Gould and Rachel replied with maniacal laughter and an elaborate defence of childless marriages.

"Well, they try," Paleologue said in the taxi back to the hotel.

"But the daughter succeeds."

At that moment Gould was not trying. "Not tonight, Rachel, I guess I've had too much booze. I just couldn't get it up."

"Give me five minutes, I'll get it up for you."

"Aw, Rachel, come on, I just don't feel like it."

"Yeah, eh? Seems to me you haven't felt like it for quite a while. Getting old, are you?"

"Lay off, Rachel."

"Getting a bit old and decrepit, are you? Can't cut the mustard anymore? Bet you can get it up for that little blonde bit, the one who's doing the Metcalf thesis, eh? Bet she doesn't have to blow you for five minutes before . . . ."

"All right!"

Gould had long been circumspect in his use of physical violence against Rachel. The night of their first anniversary he had slapped her hard enough to make her mouth bleed; she had broken his jaw with a champagne bottle. As everyone who knew her remarked at some time or other, Rachel was a big woman. So she sat in the middle of the bed, cross-legged and smirking.

After a few false starts, Gould began, speaking in an artificially calm voice: "You know, Rachel, I think the thing I most dislike about you is how you always twist things. I admit it, there is a problem between us about Sandra. I admit that I did mention I found I was attracted to her, but I mentioned it only as a curiosity: the fact that you are tall, very well-built and brunette, while she is medium height, skinny and blonde. I was wondering if this confirmed that old theory that people are attracted to types who are the opposites of their spouses. It is an intellectual question of general application. I only mentioned the case of Sandra because it was a case of such an attraction. Mild attraction, quite innocent, the sort of thing that happens, quite natural and beyond human control. What is controllable is what one does about it: in this case, absolutely nothing. I mean, I have never even been tempted to sleep with her, let alone actually try doing it." (That afternoon in his office: "They're like lemons, lovely little lemons and their tips have been dipped in . . . in the juice of sweet, black cherries, mmm. . . . ") "Look, I know jealousy is a perfectly normal emotion—just like sexual attraction—but this shouldn't mean you suspend entirely all use of your brain. And you are intelligent, Rachel, you know you are. If you were just a dumb broad there might be some excuse, but you're an intelligent and relatively sophisticated woman. I don't know, Jesus, perhaps that's the answer, that you're a woman. I know what it sounds like, but maybe women really can't generalize their experiences, maybe they always see the world in their own purely personal terms . . . no, wait, let me finish. I mean, I'm not even saying it's wrong, or that I'm right . . . Jesus Christ, you know, do you really think it's all that great being a man? Having to be sane and reasonable and . . . responsible all the fucking time? You know, I'm responsible for bringing in the cash that keeps this family going, it's my work that's going to keep a roof over our heads, that's going to send Sarah to college, that's going to provide for us in our old age. I know you'd do it if you had to or if you could earn more than I do or whatever, but the fact is that right now I am responsible and every day I walk around doing a job I don't give a damn for anymore—no, that's not true, I do care about the little private things I have—but it wouldn't matter anyway, because no matter how I feel I still have to do the job, because I am responsible. I'm not complaining, really, I'm just saying that's my life and I have to live it and if I didn't want it . . . shit, I guess I could change it. And, you know, it's been okay, I don't have to shovel shit, despite what some of my students think of my lectures, and I have a nice warm house in the wintertime and four months off in the summer and a beautiful wife whom I love very much and who loves me and a lovely little daughter that I'd give my right nut to see have a happy life, and I count my blessings and . . . so on and so on. But . . . aw shit Rachel, sometimes I just . . . I get so tired, I don't know. . . . Just sometimes it would be nice to let up, just stop and lie back and say the hell with it all, just relax, and let someone else worry about how to pay the insurance premiums and keep up the payments on the car and the house and be sure there's enough back to pay for all the Christmas presents and the whole fucking thing, just. . . . I'm not saying you don't have to work too, love, keeping the house going, taking care of Sarah, I know, taking care of me, Christ, and I know a lot of it is simple drudgery, and you get tired too, but. . . . I don't know, with me it's as if the responsibility, the whole masculine world, just drains away all the psychic energy that should be going into love-making, into caring for you in the small personal ways that . . . like not forgetting our anniversary, you know, Jesus, love, I felt so terrible about that, really I. . . .

You know, a man is supposed to be strong, he even has to appear to be strong, especially when he's scared shitless and . . . it's like you were saying, a man should have the right to cry too, and . . . ."

"I didn't say that."

"Yes you did, I remember, just this after . . . ."

It was at this point that Rachel threw a full crystal ashtray at his head and bounced out of the bedroom. At four hours it was no longer than their average fight. When it was over, they made love with much thrashing and fuss despite Gould's black eye and Rachel's bruises. She had been made to sweep out the bed and he to shampoo the coffee out of the living room carpet.

Sarah listened to it all. She was intensely curious about grown-ups, considered herself simply a grown-up in training, and was therefore willing to crouch in corners for hours in hope of learning something new. During the seventeen years she lived at home, she found out just about everything there was to find out about Gould and Rachel. "And she's going to spend the rest of her life trying to forget it all." This comment was made by Boden Rastuble, the self-styled poet whom she married when they were both nineteen. If it can be said that, while at home, the subject of her study had been a marriage, then her own could be taken as clear proof that her analysis left something to be desired. Rastuble was the sole issue from a marriage between a Bombay brothel keeper and an eight-foot-tall Arizona cowgirl named Mickey. He was a poet only for the sake of his pursuit of Sarah which lasted a day and a half. The poetry he recited to her in the Finnish (he had spent some years there as a child) was in fact nothing but long pieces inaccurately quoted from the *Kalevala* which he had been made to memorize as a schoolboy. Sarah's weakness for poets (at least until she saw a sample of their work) was notorious around the university and Rastuble managed to take her from "Hi there" to honeymoon in just over the statutory minimum time period. The uncovering of the *Kalevala* hoax (which took Sarah three weeks) meant the marriage was doomed. More serious was Rastuble's questionable ability to make verifiable contact with the real world. His remark about Sarah and her parents (made to a library assistant he was groping in the stacks

138

a week after the nuptials) was one of the few lucid remarks he made during that black time. They cohabited for three months. Then he left and she never saw him or heard of from him again. In fact, the closest connection between them occurred when Grilse had Rastuble notarize some documents for him in Beirut five years later; but Grilse did not know of the marriage. His disappearance saved Sarah a lot of trouble, for it meant that she was legally married in conditions which made four years of separation the only grounds for divorce and, if the truth be known, Sarah would have entered into one disastrous marriage a month had the law allowed it. Unable to marry, she had affairs, many affairs.

She had the perception to know herself and what she was doing to herself; but not the will to stop doing it. And in spite of herself she found excuses, as people always will.

"My fornications, as you choose to call them, Rachel, may well have become notorious. Easy come, easy go. But, in the first place, they don't seem to have hampered my academic career, do they? And in the second place, they're none of your goddamn business. And in the third place, I have no intention of following your example by chaining myself to a fool like Gould for the rest of my life."

"You're already married, Sarah. You married younger than I did."

"Legally I am married to what's-his-name, I admit it. True or not, though, the point is irrelevant. Not surprisingly, since you have never been a particularly logical person."

Rachel took her cup over to the stove and poured coffee into it. With her free hand she wiped her eyes: Dear God, how can I help my daughter?

"Sarah," she murmured, "I know you're smarter than I am, that's been obvious since you were a child. I have never denied that. . . . No, I suppose I have, but even in saying it, I knew it wasn't true. But Sarah, brains aren't everything. You're smarter than, I don't know, Paleologue, but he's happier, he runs his life better than . . . ."

"Go to hell," venomously.

Rachel hung her head, not bothering to hide the tears now. I don't care, she thought, I've given up trying to impress her with strength, I have no more power over her.

139

"I'm sorry, Sarah, I'm so sorry about that, it was so . . . arrogant, so . . . ."

"Arrogant?"

"Oh God, Sarah, whatever word you want, I don't know, I've given up defending it even to myself, I was wrong, horribly wrong. . . . "

"Jesus Christ, Rachel, you still don't understand, do you? You still think I was . . . maimed or something because you deliberately sent me off to get laid when I was only a peach-fuzz pubescent. Maimed? Hunh."

And Sarah went for a coffee, wondering why she was on the verge of tears herself and working it out: "Because Rachel hasn't understood all these years, because nobody has ever understood and when no one understands you you're alone and being alone is. . . . "

"Sarah, I. . . . "

"Maimed? Yes, in a way I was, but far worse than you think. It wasn't having my virginity taken by him," (she could never say his name) "what could possibly be wrong with having a wonderful, tender, gentle . . . oh shit, a man like that initiate you? Poor brainy, bony little Sarah-child being shown that she's a woman, what it is to be a woman. What does it matter that I thought I seduced him and found out otherwise, what does that matter? Fuck all. . . . Hunh. Fuck all: that's appropriate. Yes, I suppose I was maimed, because, obviously, I'm 'fucking all' in the, no doubt, vain hope of finding a man who measures up to a memory. Maimed? Goddamn right I'm . . . . Oh, the hell with it, Jesus, I don't want to talk about it, I'm going over to the shopping centre to get a Christmas present for Gould. What would you suggest, a book of pornographic etchings?"

"Oh Sarah!"

But Sarah was getting into her coat and walking out the door, a big, beautiful woman, with tears behind the sunglasses, her mother's daughter.

"Oh my poor Sarah . . . my Sarah . . . ."

Dead colours, the corpse colours of last year. The last of the snow in the shadows and along the bushy edges, grainy as a bad photograph. Sarah had not expected a locked gate and had

140

to leave the car at the end of the lane, to go the rest of the way in her city shoes. Fool, she thought, you might have remembered there aren't any sidewalks . . . oh, shut up, bitch. . . . Jesus, it's cold . . . .

She picked her way along, between the ruts and the patches of snow. The lane had not been maintained; for years now, only Ti-Paulo had come here and he only during the summer, too busy with work and hobbies to be much bothered with maintenance. Other things had changed: she remembered bushes between the house and the road, but not this forest.

So, she said, not quite aloud, *Nel mezzo del cammin di nostra vita,* I found myself . . . in a dark wood, lost from the direct path. . . . And that is the house in which I was . . . conceived, as she rounded the last turn and looked across to the house Dimitri and Francesca had once called their "rose-covered cottage" being, as Ti-Paulo had told Rachel almost thirty-four years ago: "in fact, an expensive piece of fast-dating flamboyance more appropriately surrounded by cactus than roses."

Well, it looks pretty dismal. Some local lawyer in charge of keeping it up and doesn't do any more than he can get away with. I suppose Ti-Paulo doesn't care as long as the house is livable. . . . And I was here that summer when I . . . was thirteen. . . . And . . . hunh, as an egg . . . shit, don't get. . . . I suppose they went swimming over there. . . . Dam's been taken care of . . . Ti-Paulo, I suppose, him . . . my . . . the man who impregnated my mother . . . hell . . . .

One step at a time, she threaded her way down to the dam and stood there and plucked idly at the clicking willow branches hanging down. Everything is so grey . . . grey and dismal and gloomy. . . . I suppose it isn't really fair, it must have been very nice that summer, will be again this summer, but right now . . . .

She was talking out loud, murmuring, as people do who are alone or lonely; she had come to see and to hear and was instead making sounds to be heard and doing things to be seen, listening to herself, watching herself, not seeing what was around her, not hearing. So it was that Naseby got quite close to her before she was aware of him.

"Oh!"

"Heh."

"I . . . uhh. . . . "

"Judo girl, heh," for Sarah had jumped into a defensive stance for just a moment. "I'll have to be careful, won't I, heh, calm down honey, calm down, no one's going to hurt you . . . ."

But Naseby (she knew him at once; it had to be him) had moved too close to her, violating those unspoken laws of distance that all people know, knowing he was violating them, that she felt violated, but thinking incorrectly that she did not know why she felt uneasy.

"Why are you backing off, why are you afraid, I'm not hurting you, why are you . . . ."

"Stuff it, mister, I know very well what you're doing and so do you. Move any closer and I'll disable you."

"A tough one, eh?"

"Very tough, Naseby."

It got him, as names always do. He stopped and looked at this person who had named him. Squinting through the thick lenses he tried to see through her pale blue sunglasses, through her grey-blue eyes, trying to make out her nature, her name. And after a minute his lips pulled back from the yellowing teeth and made the notorious Naseby leer.

"Ah yes, yes, I'm getting old, eyes going rotten, should have known you right off," relaxing now, putting his hand into the pockets of the Norfolk jacket he had scrounged out of a closet, the jacket Francesca had given Dìmitri to go with the house and the land and which Dimitri had only worn twice, "yes, there's no mistaking the figure, the hair, the ass, the tits. But mostly the legs, mostly the legs. They're better than your mother's, I think, though I haven't seen her for years. You must exercise them a lot, eh? Yes, I expect it's something to have those stems wrapped around your waist and pumping the juice out of you, yes. Your mother was just the same, break a man's back if you didn't watch out, nice lay she was, but tire you out in no time if you weren't in good shape, yes, really take it out of you, she could. Heh. Bet you like it that way too, eh, with the mouth, yes, you've got the lips for it, just like your mother, gobble anything, she would, figured it wasn't really dirty as long as she had her clothes on, real maniac for it, did

142

the whole football team the last year in school as a reward for winning some piece of silver, yes, a real cheerleader your mother was, yes, can see her now, clear as I see you, yes, crawling along that stinking locker room floor, crawling through the sweat socks and the jockstraps, right down the line she went, creaming at the mouth like one of those French pastries with the filling coming out, yes, you're your mother's daughter, sure enough, except for the brains, no one ever called poor Rachel bright, the opposite in fact, but you've got brains, I can see it in the eyes, yes, and you know it too, eh, you know it, yes. Don't do you much good though, do they? Oh yes, I can see from the clothes that you're doing all right for yourself, got a small fortune on your back, you have, and that was one hell of an expensive engine I heard stopping at the end of the lane a while ago, yes, you're healthy enough in the bankbook, all right, but it doesn't do you a damn bit of good, does it? No, there's no escaping that itchy crotch, is there? Mommy's little girl, and all the brains in the world aren't worth a damn, because when you're dripping into your drawers you're nothing but an animal, eh, crazy for a big hunk of meat and all the big words in the dictionary don't matter fuck all. Yes, fuck all, yes you've tried that too and you can't get enough of it. Drives you crazy, doesn't it? Doesn't help your temper, either, one miserable big bitch of a woman I bet you are, eh? Yes, funny how these things come back to you, I remember a few stories about you, one little bitch of a kid you were, real little prodigy, shooting your mouth off, big words, read books and made sure everyone knew it, too, real smart-ass little bitch of a kid you were. Now who told me that, I wonder? Funny, you know, haven't seen any of that crew for . . . ohh, twenty, twenty-five years, been wondering about them this winter, I've . . . borrowed this place . . . between engagements, heh, lonely out here, think about those snotty bastards, got lots of time for thinking these days, and. . . . Yes, it was one of them told me about you, gave me the low-down, can't get much lower than you've been, heh, yes, Ti-Paulo, that's who it was, nasty little prick but that only fits, eh, considering his . . . relationship to you, heh, but I can see you know all about that, yes, and . . . yes, that's why you're here, come to look the place over, see where your slut of a

143

mother spread her legs for you, heh, but no, it wasn't Ti-Paulo who gave me the real goods on you, it must have been, yes, that arrogant, conceited bastard Paleologue, yes, by God, that's who it was, old P., sitting in the old tavern back home, sitting there and smirking and telling me about Rachel's bitchy little daughter . . . ."

Sarah's scream began with a startled, strangled gasp. It rose slowly in tone and volume, rose through the air as her face turned up to the sky. Her shoulders slumped and her arms fell limp and her purse fell to the ground with a soft plop and still the scream rose in tone and volume until it filled the air all about. Perhaps it was this fullness which made it seem almost peaceful, almost serene as it hung over the meadow, hung like smoke under the bare trees and seemed to persist long after it had faded away (as the smell of wood smoke lingers in the air) seemed to persist even after Sarah had slipped to the ground, her body lying askew on a patch of snow.

The scream had an oddly hypnotic effect on Naseby, something as new and surprising to him as his terror upon being named. He was full of awe at the power of the effect. He had always been able to get people, to wound them with words; but he had never managed such an effect. It gave him something beyond mere satisfaction, something much closer to ecstasy, as if he were a violinist who, after a lifetime of practice, had performed with such completeness, such purity that the performance was the sum of his life, all his art in one perfect act. In that ecstasy Naseby ceased to be Naseby and became both less and more than himself: his lust, his avarice, his envy fell away from him and there remained only the ecstasy which vibrated with the crystalline purity of the soul of a saint in the desert.

And Sarah, in her scream, was insane. It was not that she believed Paleologue had said such things about her, for she knew Naseby by his reputation, she knew he was a canny liar and his attack on her through her mother had shown her how ingeniously inventive he was.

She had a vision of a cathedral. She was standing in the nave and looking up toward the high arches, when she noticed that some stones were beginning to fall away, drifting down toward her. "Hey, I'd better watch it, one of those stones might hit me." The falling stones were a mere curiosity, really, for they came down so slowly that she was easily able to step aside. Then she was stopped by a new sight: first one, then another, then all the pillars buckled and crumbled and she knew the cathedral was collapsing around her. She was still safe, for she would be able to step out of the way, it was only a vision. She knew Paleologue had not said those things about her, but now she put the question: "But what if he had?" and the floor of the cathedral gave way beneath her and she and her cathedral went tumbling into the pit.

The appearance of the vision and her progress from curiosity through fear to terror to utter despair took only a moment, the time she took forming the notion of the question to the stating of the question, and as she stated it, "But what if he had?" the floor gave way and her lungs gasped to suck in air and her mind collapsed.

Every excuse, every evasion disappeared. If she could form the question of doubt, she could doubt everything: I have never known myself, I was a little bitch, I was never loved, I have never loved, I am a whore, I am insane, I am wrong, I am stupid, I am an animal, I am garbage, I am scum, I am filthy, I am pure evil, I am nothing . . . .

The mind cannot bear these thoughts; to protect itself it stops working and waits.

When Sarah regained consciousness she was sane again. She saw that her vision was not true; but she remembered the horror and desolation of despair: this could come again (did several times over the next few years, but never with the same power of this first, sudden, unexpected attack) and the only way of protecting herself was to numb her mind to many things. Perhaps later she could begin to question herself again, perhaps later.

For the moment, though, she had to protect herself from Naseby who, as she regained consciousness, was fumbling under her skirt.

The great power of the well-trained judoist is that the skill is habit. Perception of attack, perception of position, selection of act, action: all these can occur with next to no conscious thought. Sarah was not much interested in Naseby or in what he was doing; she had been handled by too many men to care; but he was leaning over her body and she wanted to get up. So she moved him. She did it nonchalantly, negligently, like a drawing room hostess gesturing boors aside. Naseby was kneeling; and then he was tumbling forward over her body and rolling down the bank of the dam to the water of the pool. As Sarah's mind had numbed itself against the pain of her vision, Naseby's mind numbed itself against the pain of his broken spine. He came to rest along the edge of the water, the left side of his body in the water, the right side on the bank. For a moment he held his face above the surface and gazed at his reflection; then the numbness swept over him and his face fell forward.

Sarah had forgotten him before he stopped rolling. The obstacle was removed; she stood up and walked away. She did not turn around, for it was not what she was going from, but what she was going to: Sarah was going home.

Back in her apartment it took her only a moment to find the diary, though she had not seen it for years, had not read it since she had written it. A school notebook with hard-board covers, black, smaller than she remembered, three-fourths filled with handwriting smaller than she remembered, not so neat and legible as she expected. She read it slowly, mouthing the words, numbly at first, having to re-read many sentences, almost memorizing the lines before she could hold them together in her mind. As she read, the tears trickled down her cheeks: it was only natural.

When she finished the diary, she fell back on the bed and stared at the ceiling and smoked cigarettes. She felt exhausted: the country air? After a while she ran out of cigarettes but was too tired to reach over the edge of the bed for the other pack in her purse. A while after that she was too tired to think and by five in the morning she was too tired to cry.

She lay there while the room brightened. She was glad the sun was coming up because she was cold and too tired to pull the covers over herself. She smiled at the sunlight. After an hour it would make her warm. Waiting for the sun to make her warm was so much easier than pulling the covers over herself.

When she was warm she moved. She rolled her legs to the edge of the bed and over and sat up and grinned at the patch of sunlight on the wall. Then she undressed and showered and put on clean clothes. She was humming tunelessly, idiotically as she put on her coat and went out the door. The sky was overcast now, but she was glad because the sun would have hurt her eyes.

"Why Sarah, what are you doing here?"

"Scrounging breakfast. Any to spare?"

"Of course, sit down, the coffee's almost done . . . ."

Gould came in a few minutes later, scratching his belly through the parting in his robe and complaining about the toothpaste being squeezed from the wrong end of the tube.

"She's always been a slut, Sarah. The first time I ever saw her, the end of her bra strap was sticking out of her dress, she . . . ."

"Listen to him, will you, calls me a slut, but ask him what he was doing gawking down the front of my dress, eh? I'll tell you what he was doing, copping a few cheap thrills, a dirty old man at twenty-two, and still is, why just the other day . . . ."

"Damn it Rachel, that doesn't count, you . . . ."

"Listen to him, Sarah, it's the same all the . . . ."

"Momma . . . Poppa . . . ."

For the first time in years there was dead silence in that house: Sarah had come home.

None of them really knew what to do about it. Rachel snuffled into a handkerchief and Gould cleared his throat and pretended he was only rubbing the sleep from his eyes and Sarah bit her lip and kept biting her lip until she couldn't stop herself and then she cried and Rachel cried and they held each other and cried together until they laughed and Gould coughed some more and then began to babble:

"Sweet Jesus, look at the time, I've got a class in half an hour, come on Rachel, hop it. Christ Almighty, just what you'd expect in a house full of women, I don't know how I've stood it, all these years . . . ."

7

Walk

They walked west across fields covered with snow, Paleologue and Gussie. At the edge of their farm they slipped through the fringe of pines and crossed the road. The fields before them rose gently, a blaze of light under a clean blue sky. Paleologue stood by the fence rail which was still above the snow and offered his hand to his wife. As she lifted her leg over, he goosed her.

"Ahk!"

"Careful of the voice."

"Old goat."

She lifted his sunglasses and peered into his eyes. "Is this perhaps the onset of your second childhood, my love?" Reaching up to rub noses, "Or could it be," softly, "you're still in your first?"

Then she goosed him.

"Ow, hey, careful, I'm a poet, those things are vital to me, the future of poetry is in your hands, the soul of the nation, the . . . ."

Chattering, hand in hand, they set off across the fields of light.

There had been several heavy falls of snow that winter. The

week before there had been a day of misting rain and now the snow had a thick crust on it, strong enough to support them in most places. It was the crusty snow that had decided them on walking. The crust and the sun rising into the clear, pale sky.

They walked hand in hand, talking. Sometimes it seemed to them that they had done nothing for forty years but talk. They talked when they met, when they became lovers, whispered through the marriage ceremony to the annoyance of the minister, through the reception to the annoyance of the guests, and on and on to the annoyance of many, to the delight of others, and their own enchantment.

They met at the launching party of Paleologue's third book. It was the party of the week, a freak because he was still a nobody. Gussie arrived after eleven straight from the show that was making her the toast of the town. Katherine Hepburn and Bea Lillie with sex they were saying; the looks, the legs, the brains, the wit, she had it all, a new star rising. She came with a movie actor, all beefcake, and left him at the door. She ran into Paleologue at the bar.

"Good evening," she chirruped, "I've just arrived. Who's the sensitive plant whose soul we're supposed to be celebrating?"

"That fellow over there," Paleologue replied, indicating the fat, fatuous, red-headed drama critic of *The Times*.

"My, my, wasn't I mistaken? He doesn't look either sensitive or soulful."

"Oh, but the woman next to him is; very sensitive and as soulful as they come," the woman being the equally fat and equally fatuous wife of his publisher.

"Really? She doesn't look it either."

"Oh yes, take my word for it. Or read about her in the papers. That's Gussie Trevelyan, blazing new star of that world of tinsel and make-believe called the stage."

"No, I'm afraid I only read the Editorial and Foreign Affairs pages. Do tell me about her," and poured her martini into Paleologue's breast pocket. "Ohh! Pardon me," she cried.

"My clumsiness, I'm sure," and tipped an inch and a half of cigar ash into the front of her dress.

"Akh!"

"No, no, let me," and made as if to plunge his hand down her dress.

"Damn poets," she fumed, brushing the hand away, "you're all the same, think because you can blather on about stars and roses you're absolutely the world's greatest lovers when in fact . . . ."

"We should be hacking out vulgar praises of snot-nosed little actresses who carry around their brains in their brassieres."

"Pfui. Never wear the ghastly things."

"All the more reason for me to get the ash out of there. Might cauterize your frontal lobe."

"You do that, I'll get the olive out of your pocket, I do love olives. Do you love . . . eeek! You're tickling . . . ."

It was at this moment that a cunning photographer popped up from behind a potted palm and snapped the picture that added at least six months to the run of Gussie's play and put Paleologue's book on the best seller list, the first book of poetry to make it in at least a decade. Their combined extra earnings gave them a six month honeymoon wandering around the globe and paid in full for the farm that was to continue all these years their favourite private place.

They had been spending a long midwinter at the farm and now they were going to the train and back to the city where Gussie had a new play in rehearsal and Paleologue was to receive an award. They had until evening to get to the station but had given themselves all day because of their age and because, although the fields looked flat, they rose slightly for the first half of the journey, then fell toward the town. The wind moved over the fields, light and trailing, bracing and comfortable. After an hour they were skirting a woodlot, so they stopped for a cup of coffee and a slab of chocolate from Paleologue's backpack.

"Mmm, good coffee."

He leaned his head against her shoulder.

"Yes, good coffee," she replied, "and warm sun."

She stroked his head; it's all right, now, it's all right, don't worry about it, but she knew it wasn't all right and it never would be. It would go away in just a moment and at worst it had never lasted more than two years, two hellish years, admittedly, but it had always gone away and things had gotten better again. She had named it his devil, at times his angel, and she suspected she was the only one who had ever seen it. She had cursed it, blessed it, loved, hated, pondered it but, out of some sense of propriety, had never asked him about it. It came at odd moments: the usual early hours of the morning, at parties, after some hours of paradise on a deserted beach. It came unexpectedly, when he was deep in a mystery novel or out with her window-shopping for a new dress. It looked like a loosening of the muscles. His eyes lost their focus, his body slumped slightly, his mouth fell slack. When she spoke he would not hear her. He was lost somewhere out there, or somewhere in there, but lost. She first met it a year and half after the wedding. She was passing the door of the study and heard his voice, quiet and far away: "I'm so tired, God, so tired." She stopped and was about to ask him, on reflex, to ask what he had said, before she understood. She caught herself in time and crept away and cried. After an hour she got up and made him a spectacular supper. To her surprise he came down the stairs humming and singing, danced her about the room, sniffed the pots, kissed her from head to foot and suggested they go out dancing that night. "What have you been smoking up there?" "The steppes of Russia." "Good day's work?" and kicked herself: his pause was so slight that only a lover could have noticed it, a moment of utter desolation in his eyes, but the memory of that moment could still make her shiver. For the eyes she saw were not the eyes of her husband. "Great day's work," he had replied and danced over to the stove again. She knew then that he could go away from her and come back again to arrange words of the English language in certain ways. She had married a poet.

When they had the thermos packed away, Paleologue got to his feet. "Off we go, old lady."

And they got up and didn't look at each other.

As the sun rose to the zenith, light cloud slid in high from the west. The sun still shone through, but paler now, pale yellow, a more appropriate winter sun, and the fields rising gently before them now glowed gently in the pale light.

Gussie and Paleologue had seen three kinds of birds and a couple of rabbits. They had argued once again through the ethics of Paleologue's accepting the award. It was a medal and a cheque for several thousand dollars, the nation's highest award for writers. He was, in fact, a decade or two overdue for it, so that Gussie considered the award almost an insult.

"Nonsense, dumpling . . ."

"Don't you dare call me that when we're arguing."

" . . . since my first book came out I have been married to you with all your fame and vulgar money and . . ."

"Goddamnit, that shouldn't count!"

" . . . I do make money myself . . ."

"You've been penalized for your success."

" . . . and there has always been someone else who, if not quite as good as I am . . ."

"False modesty! Understatement!"

" . . . at least needed the money more than I did. Very few poets make anything from . . . ."

"Very neat, I'm sure, but. . . ." And she pointed out that acceptance would imply approval of the government's policies on a number of issues, policies they thought wrong. Paleologue's counter-argument was that he disagreed with the government, he didn't want to overthrow it and in that case if he waited for perfection he would wait forever. "Besides," he added, "in some way or other, the award does come from the people of the country and I am proud . . ."

"Jesus Christ, love!"

" . . . proud, I say, to be honoured by them in some way other than royalty statements. Besides, what about your Oscar?"

"Unfair, unfair, my agent made me do it, and besides, I was young and ignorant and my brain was completely muddled by my recent marriage to a rather plausible poet who has about as much understanding of politics as an ostrich."

Paleologue spoke at length on the political perceptions of the ostrich. "Why, it's very name is derived from the German for 'Eastern Empire.' That is, 'Österreich' or Austria . . . ."

Gussie had been terrified of what the war would do to him. While he was in reserve he wrote her travelogue and thought letters with a poem each time. But during the seven months he was at the front, the letters, when they came, were horrible to read. No travelogue, no reflections and certainly no poems, not the long, neat, weekly letters, but a single page cheatingly filled with large, sloppy sprawl. Meanderings like:

"It is cloudy and cold but we are comfortable. I have a new pair of socks. They are warm. Glad your play is going well, isn't it. I can smell pine trees. They are all around. The pines. We eat soon. It is a nice, hot stew. I like cigarettes. I am happy. I miss you."

Then when he was invalided back home he seemed the same. It was almost a year from the time he had been wounded and the war was almost over. It was several years before he would talk about it, about the real thing, even to her. He never talked about it to anyone else and wrote only a few bad poems about it, all later destroyed. But from the time he returned, he seemed the same as before he went away.

It had something to do with balance. Paleologue the acrobat. He could see the good and the bad in all things and was neither impressed with the one nor disgusted by the other. From the time they bought the farm, Paleologue had been working on the house. He had spent years with mallet and chisel cutting decorations into the beams and bannisters. He took down the plaster and put up new coats whenever Ti-Paulo came to visit. Ti-Paulo paid for his visits by painting on real *buon fresco.* There were built-in bookcases, oaks planted on the land, rows of Lombardy poplar, things built and growing and put there to last and flourish beyond his own lifetime. But Paleologue said:

"Permanence? Of course I don't believe in permanence, it's an illusion. You never know what might happen. Look, I've renovated to prevent fire, rot and termites, there are no floods on high ground, we own all the oil, mineral and timber rights, I see no possibility of anyone building a highway or railway through here, and only a madman would want to build a housing development around here. The land is too hilly for an airport. So, sure, I've done everything humanly possible to make the place permanent. Hell, we're famous enough that it might even be of interest to the Historical Sites Bureau. But that still isn't permanence. We have no children, there might be a civil war, a mad arsonist, vandals, lightning . . . ."

But he could be bribed into the best of humour with a cup of coffee. It was a trick Gussie used all the time. His eyes lit up. He cradled the cup in both hands and sucked in the aroma. He sipped, savoured, sighed. So with all the little pleasures. The sunrise was a miracle, a summer breeze, falling rain, a blizzard, people on the street, a poem, Gussie, a walk across winter fields.

"You know, I was thinking the other day how lucky we've been," Gussie remarked as they stopped at the height of land. "I was reading Herodotus again; I had forgotten how chaotic and accidental life can be."

They looked out over a valley of farmland with the open fields under snow, woodlots spotted about, lines of trees between them, trees along the roads, the big brushes of willows along the river. As they ate their sandwiches they stared over the landscape, distracted by its seeming peace.

"Yes," replied Paleologue.

Where Paleologue was, he was in many costumes; Gussie was always and all ways Gussie. Together, he was the landscape in which she walked and all the people she met there.

They had managed by knowing the way through. While Paleologue was overseas, Gussie had stayed in town and worked almost continually. Gould and Rachel came to see her once and she chattered about a new Ti-Paulo above the fireplace. Finally they asked about Paleologue and she rattled on without pausing:

"Oh I sent him a photograph of the painting before I bought it he's an ogre about that sort of thing I remember once in Paris I bought one of those little watercolours of Notre Dame and when I got it home he took one look at it then calmly wrapped it up and mailed it to N. . . . " (The reviewer who had criticized three of his books.) They were leaving about six when she opened the door to her greasy and smirking male lead. He poured himself a proprietary drink, put his feet up on an expensive coffee table (a wedding gift from Dimitri and Francesca) and insulted Gould's pipe and Rachel's shoes. On the street they fumed about the treachery.

"I don't care if she is an actress, she kissed him like a lover."

"If that bitch is sleeping with that slimy . . . ."

"Who cares about a piece of strange now and then?" Paleologue had been heard to say. "Adultery is so trivial," she used to say. "I might leave him because he didn't wash his feet, but never because he slept with another woman. Or man." "I've got bigger fish to fry." This could have been either one speaking. "Bigger fish indeed." Gussie had known very well what Gould and Rachel were saying and wished they were still in the room so she could say: "Listen, Jesus Christ, you two are amazing, you really are. Does your reading stop in 1899? Do you really think that adultery has anything to do with marriage? God!" Gussie had a temper and was willing to use it as a knife, scalpel or bludgeon as the occasion required. Paleologue was rarely aroused enough to bother with anger. But when Gould wrote him about the greasy male lead, Paleologue, on garrison duty, replied with a post card: "Mind your own goddamn business."

Gussie poured the last of the coffee into their cups and they sat sipping as the meal settled. They were polite to their bodies and their bodies gave them the possibility of calm minds.

"Doing things," she said. "We have managed because we damn well have done things. And we have . . . I don't know . . . somehow we've . . . been inclined to do what was possible and also what was right. That takes a hell of a lot of luck." And after a pause: "It also takes knowledge and . . . hunh . . . the famous arrogance."

"Hardly so, my chuff. You stand on top of a cliff by the sea and take photographs. After a while you pause to watch a seagull wheeling below you and you think . . . hmm . . . many things about it. But ho! with a negligent shrug you can throw your camera or yourself over the edge, actions that no amount of thought or luck or arrogance can reverse. Hmm?"

"Oh shit, don't be so narrow. To think is to act. And there are reversible actions and actions which are not violent. Like drinking your coffee."

"Oh act-fact. Action has about it the violence of fact. Consider Edward the Confessor, hmm? Sat around contemplating the kingdom of Heaven and his own kingdom fell into chaos. Or something simpler, perhaps, the scholar among his books. His wife may commit suicide from neglect. But consider also the exploration of the jungle behind his eyes: this is also action. (Careful, you'll spill your coffee. No, lay off Gussie, let me finish.) The scholar explores his jungle, eh, and then he must draw maps: the putting of pen to paper, this is the violent one, the look on his face after the first line. He has drawn it so and this way or that. Selection is violence, hmm?"

"Damn it, Paleologue, you always get coy. You know very well . . . ."

And so on through coffee and down the gentle slope of three fields under the high, pale clouds, under the pale sun glimmering through, glimmering pale yellow.

Gussie and Paleologue kept moving; in their lives they always kept moving. No one had ever locked either of them in a closet. "Miss Trevelyan, you have established yourself as the first comedienne of the stage. With *Stuff and Nonsense* nearing the end of its run, have you another script under consideration?"

"Yes, just this morning I accepted the part of the Duchess of Malfi at the University of . . ." or "the second garbage can in L's new thing . . ." naming the blackest mind in several centuries, or "retiring for a year to learn dressmaking . . ." quite seriously, and did so.

"Look," she explained once to a serious interviewer, "it's harder to hit a moving target, right. So the next thing I'm doing is the lead in the next FBN spectacular . . . yes, it's a big budget . . . Christ, love, call the doctor, I think he's had a heart attack. . . ." FBN was Fly-by-Nite Productions, Naseby's sexploitation company. Gussie did the role and lived because she had sanity and a team of sharp lawyers. She lived because Paleologue understood, because she could afford to examine her sanity.

The movie began as a joke. Naseby forced his presence

upon them at one of Ti-Paulo's vernissages. He complimented Paleologue insincerely on his latest book, leered down Gussie's neckline. It should have been a can of worms with a fight, tears, dramatic exits. But they had been together in the world for six years and smiled and held hands.

The suggestion of a movie came as a half joke from Naseby; they went along with him for half the joke of it. Naseby said he'd call tomorrow at noon to go over the arrangements and they wandered off to look at the pictures. It was not until the next morning over a prodigally expensive breakfast on the sunny terrace of their hotel suite that Gussie brought it up.

"Well, what the hell is going on?"

"You're never as safe as you think you are."

"Would you mind if I did it?"

"Yes . . . ."

"Yes, but?"

"Yes, but. But what is the issue?"

"The issue is whether you want your wife going in front of a rented camera to perform unnatural acts with Naseby's studs and whores."

"The issue is what you and I and we together want. That makes it a bit more complicated."

"Look lover," she said, "we were wrong. We've beaten a lot of people. We've beaten contracts, laws, customs, habits. We've done everything we wanted to do because we knew ourselves and ourselves together, what we had to gain or lose. But this time we don't know for sure."

He argued for a few changes in this stand, but largely he agreed. So they sat down to think through what it was all about. They decided Naseby was irrelevant: he never went into anything without being sure (perhaps too sure?) he could win. In his own terms Naseby would win either way: if she did the movie he would plan on making a fortune; if she refused, he had beaten her, them. The morality of it was also irrelevant: they were artists. They further agreed they were equally involved. He had to write the script, she had to perform it. They valued their marriage equally, each other equally, needed an equal measure of will.

She concluded with: "It's like climbing a mountain that has

been climbed before, there's no glory in it. We risk our lives because to take risks is healthy for the soul and for no other reason whatsoever. Right? If we don't climb the mountain it's like drawing a line around the foot of the mountain and saying, 'This mountain is not to be climbed.' "

"Let's get the boots on, then."

They shook hands on it and went inside to make love. When Naseby called they said they were agreed in principle and he could see their lawyers and agents about the terms. Once agreed and understood, they went into the project with determination and the most improbable results. Paleologue produced a fascinating script, Gussie insisted on choosing her own technicians and editor and all together they charmed Naseby's cast into taking direction from them. The shooting took two weeks and by the end of it Naseby was a nervous wreck. And the movie was a critical success. It played long runs at the art houses but, despite its unprecedented filth, flopped at the skin houses. Naseby's painstakingly assembled network of stubble-cheeked, cigar chomping, bum-pinching contacts deserted him wholesale, generally without paying the fees. But he discovered much worse trouble in his own office: through a complicated series of clauses in the various contracts, Paleologue and Gussie were entitled to something like 85% of the profits. Through a number of friends' companies they had supplied all the film stock, camera rental, distribution, props, catering, costumes, make-up, development and advertising. Naseby was thus responsible for all the bills, but entitled to amost none of the modest but quite real profits. The shock of defeat badly unsettled him and he never again had the rather flippant confidence he needed to carry out schemes which would have been child's play to him before. His slow decline through the years brought him debauchery, prison, poverty and at the end a cold, wet death.

"Poor man," said Gussie sadly. "To die alone like that."

They came to the river road. If they followed it to the right they would come to a bridge and so across to the railway station in the town they could glimpse through the willows where the river turned.

"How does the river look?"

Paleologue clambered to the top of the snowbank on the far side of the road and scanned down the last gentle slope to the river. Low grey cloud had rolled in from the west, low under the earlier thin dome darkening the sky, bringing a sense of evening before its time.

"The river is certainly safe, but we're going to have snow in a few minutes."

"The hell with the snow, I'm damned if I'm going to take to the road after this distance."

Paleologue grinned and reached a hand down to her. They paused at the top of the bank, judging the lie of the land, the thickness of the elder clumps, the best place to get onto the river. He nodded and she nodded and they set off hand in hand down the long field. After a few minutes the first big flakes floated by them, big flakes which deadened the air around them so they walked through silence and the illusion of light in the gloom.

"The silence, the terror and the comfort."

"Jesus! Copy it down, the women's mags will love it."

"No, a gift to the day. If you don't give a few away, you find you have none to sell."

"You couldn't sell that one at a church bazaar."

"Watch your lip or you'll be selling your own story to a confession magazine."

" 'My Husband is a Poet—Must I suffer his Beatings for the Sake of Art?' "

"More like 'I am a Bitch—Do I deserve a Fat Lip?' "

They talked about the poems he had written over the mid-winter. Gussie thought they were very good, better than anything he had done in ten years.

"That one about winter nights, how does it end?"

He quoted the last few lines to her.

"I like that so much, the changes it goes through to get there make it very broad somehow."

He kissed her cold cheek and murmured in her ear and they stopped a few moments, young lovers again.

Now they were on the river ice and the willows deepened the silence and the dark.

"I know, instead of going all the way down to the marina, let's climb out at Vimy Park, hmm?"

"Why not?"

" 'Why not?' the man says. When I think of all the things that's gotten me into over the years . . . ."

"And what things that's gotten into you, eh?"

"That's none of your business. Hunh. And what about Chi-chi?" referring to his ill-conceived passion for a girl trumpeter. "At least a french hornist, my love."

Chatter, chatter, along the frozen river as the snow fell silently around.

Get up in the morning, pull on yesterday's clothes, instant coffee in a dirty cup, smoke a cigarette. In other times, other places, Gussie's acting, his poetry, failed: she became a whore, a druggie, he died young of disease and failure. But those were other places, other times.

In the bright dining car almost empty at third call, Paleologue and Gussie now with indoor clothes leaned toward each other and kissed over the white linen. A red rose floated in a glass bowl. They smiled at their reflections in the window and could not see the snow-covered countryside they passed through. Gussie glanced about to see if anyone was paying them any attention, then shifted forward in her chair.

"Higher," she purred, "Yes, higher."

THE NEW CANADIAN LIBRARY LIST